THE CUB SCOUT MYSTERY

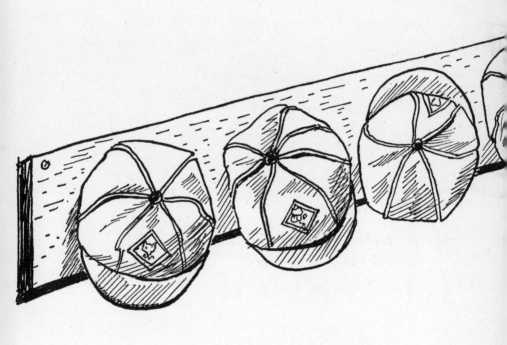

DOUBLEDAY & COMPANY, INC.

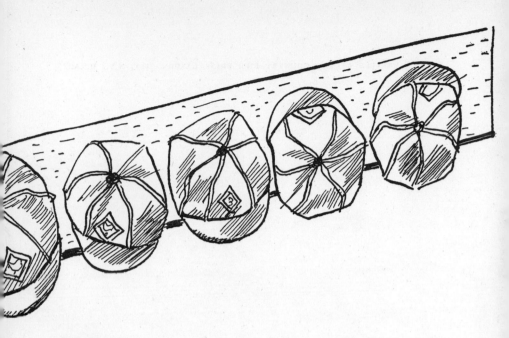

The
CUB SCOUT
Mystery

BY DOROTHY STERLING

Illustrated by Paul Galdone

GARDEN CITY, NEW YORK, 1953

PRINTED AT THE COUNTRY LIFE PRESS, GARDEN CITY, N.Y., U.S.A.

FOR PETER AND ANNE

CONTENTS

1

"Peter Howard, Bear badge, one silver arrow . . . Robert Hennessey, Bobcat pin . . . Thomas Burton, Wolf badge, gold arrow . . . Philip Sloane, three silver arrows on his Lion . . ."

Mr. Thompson, Cubmaster of the Huntsville Pack, read on and on through the list of names, pausing long enough for each boy to walk up to the front of the meeting room to receive his award and deliver a snappy salute. The audience of Cub Scouts and their parents steadily clapped. When

11

Tom Woodward, who had just moved to Huntsville, won two badges and Bill White, the smallest Cub in the Pack, marched proudly up for a Wolf badge and four arrows, the applause grew loud and some boys stamped their feet.

The awards seemed endless tonight. Eager for the games which were next on the program, the Cubs began to poke an elbow or knee in the direction of their neighbors. Whispers grew to a steady rumble of voices and some friendly wrestling started in the back of the room.

Holding up his fingers in the V sign which meant "Silence," Mr. Thompson looked down at his paper, then turned it over, a puzzled expression on his face. "Den Two," he called. "Where are your achievements? I only find one of your names on the list."

In the sudden hush, all heads turned to stare at Den Two. Eight reddening faces were grouped around a blue-and-gold banner which announced to the world that they were the Blackhawk Braves. When the silence became uncomfortable, Chuck Watson slowly pulled himself to his feet. Chuck

12

was the tallest boy in the Den and the best baseball player. Last month the boys had elected him Denner and he felt that he must answer for them to the assembled Pack.

"What's the trouble, Chuck?" Mr. Thompson asked. "You fellows were the Pack leaders last year."

Chuck, busily whispering a few minutes before, now looked down at his freshly polished shoes and could find nothing to say. "I d-d-don't know," he finally managed to stutter.

As he dropped into his chair, Bob Scherman raised his hand. Bob was Chuck's best friend, catcher to his pitcher, and Assistant Denner of Den Two. Where Chuck was tall and blond, Bob was broad and dark. And where Chuck was, Bob was sure to be.

At a nod from Mr. Thompson, he tried to explain. "We've been playing baseball every afternoon. Chuck's got a new curve none of us can hit and——"

"I'm glad to hear about the new curve." Mr. Thompson smiled. "I hope you're going to find

13

some time for Cub achievements though. Most of you fellows will be old enough to be Scouts next year." Then, turning his head to include the whole Pack, "Okay, boys," he called. "Everybody line up for the three-legged race. All Dens in the back of the room."

As if his signal had released them from prison, forty blue-uniformed boys jumped up, slid chairs back, pushed, shoved, and scrimmaged until they had made their way to the rear of the meeting room. Murmurs rose to shrieks and catcalls, and balls and caps were tossed in the air. Just as it seemed that the smaller boys and watching parents might be trampled in the stampede, Mr. Thompson put two fingers in his mouth for an ear-piercing whistle. As suddenly as the uproar had started, it stopped.

"Okay, fellows," his voice boomed out. "Line up. First race."

Den Two was holding a hurried, unhappy conference. "Gosh," Chuck kept saying, "we've been working hard on Cub stuff. It's just since baseball started." "Gosh," Bob loyally agreed.

14

Andy Hobbs took over the discussion. Andy was angry, so angry that his close-cropped red hair fairly bristled and the freckles on his nose seemed about to pop off. Andy was seldom picked for anything better than center field in baseball, but he was full of ideas. Good ideas too, the Den said. Andy wasn't angry at Mr. Thompson. It was the behavior of Den One he objected to. "Did you hear them laughing at us?" he demanded. "Just because they got more awards. We've got to show them, those—those—those Cheyenne Chowderheads," he finished on a triumphant note.

Everyone was sure that "they" had to be shown. Everyone but Sam Roth. Sam was no good at baseball at all. During team games he spent his time in the outfield watching birds or hunting beetles. His team mates would never forget when he was hit on the head by a long fly as he stooped to catch a grasshopper. "Got a fly on your head, Sam?" they still called when they wanted to tease. But Sam was good at secret codes and telling the names of trees and making campfires. He had finished more Cub achievements than anyone else, and when he talked

15

the boys usually listened. This time, Sam thought Mr. Thompson was right. "We let Den One get way ahead of us," he pointed out.

Before the argument had a chance to grow heated, there was a second whistle from Mr. Thompson. "Let's win some races," Chuck fiercely insisted as they fell into line.

Den Two, grimly determined, won the three-legged race. Den Two won the crab race. Den Two won the basketball relay. Den Two won "Simon Says Do This." Even little Jamie, who could usually be counted on to fall behind, had put on some extra steam. And in the final event of the evening Chuck, with his lower lip sucked between his teeth and a lock of straw-colored hair drooping over his eye, was the last boy standing in the Indian endurance contest.

After the fathers on the Pack Committee added up the scores, Mr. Thompson announced the winners: Den Two first, Den One second, Den Three third. "Good work, Den Two," he congratulated them. "Glad to see you're trying. Now put some of that energy into next month's Cub project.

"For our June meeting, boys," he explained to the group, "we're going to have reports on Know Your Neighborhood. Each Den will visit a different place in Huntsville and tell us about it. You can work out a skit or an exhibit or give us some speeches, but we'll want to know all about what you've seen."

"Where do we go?" "What do we do?" some of the boys called out. Mr. Thompson consulted his paper. "Your Den Mothers have all the instructions, but here's the list. Den One goes to the firehouse. Chief Whelan expects you Monday afternoon. He says you can slide down the poles and maybe he'll take you to a real fire."

Holding up his hand to stop the cheers from Den One's corner, he continued, "Den Three will visit the police station. Half of you will go out in radio cars and half will stay in the station to see how the desk sergeant handles the calls as they come in. Den Four, you will be guests of the mayor at City Hall."

The Blackhawk Braves, who a moment before had been holding their heads up proudly, now

17

looked worried. "What about us?" they wanted to know.

"Oh, did I forget Den Two?" Mr. Thompson teased. "I was saving you for the last. Den Two is going to the office of the Huntsville *Enterprise* to

give us a report on how a newspaper is published."

A chorus of groans from Den Two almost drowned out the good cheer in other parts of the meeting room. Almost, but not quite.

Mr. Thompson's eyebrows lifted. "What's the matter? Does somebody have a question?"

Andy Hobbs's red head popped up. "Jeepers, Mr. Thompson, what kind of report can you do on an old newspaper office? Everybody's got an excit-

ing job but us." He sat down in disgust, his fellow Braves scowling agreement.

"Now see here, boys." Mr. Thompson's voice was firm but not unfriendly. "I gave you the toughest assignment because you're the oldest Cubs. You're going to find plenty of interesting things at *The Enterprise*. It's one of the best newspapers in the state. It started way back before the Civil War."

But the Blackhawk Braves refused to be consoled. Studying their downcast faces, Mr. Thompson's tone grew sharper. "Den Two," he pointed out, "you've slipped from first place in the Pack to last. Even the boys in Den Four who only joined the cubs this year are ahead of you now. Let's see some real work this month to improve your record."

2

"The worst Den in the Pack," Mrs. Watson scolded as the boys assembled on Monday for their weekly meeting in her basement. "The worst Den, and that makes me the worst Den Mother."

Eight pairs of eyes which a moment before had been staring hungrily at the bottles of orange soda and plates of doughnuts in the center of the table looked up in horror.

Andy was the first to break the silence. "Oh no," he assured her, "you're the best Den Mother."

"Why, you can pitch as well as Chuck," Bob interrupted.

"Gee whiz"—Jamie's voice rose to an indignant squeak—"you know games even the boys don't know. No other Den ever had a scavenger hunt till you started them."

"Den Four doesn't do anything but play hide-and-seek all afternoon," Sam pointed out.

Only Chuck was quiet. After all, it was his mother they were talking about. "What are we going to do about it?" he asked when they had all spoken their pieces. "The honor"—and he made his voice sound like a radio announcer—"of the Blackhawk Braves is at stake."

"The honor of the Blackhawk Braves won't be worth much if the tribe starves to death," Mrs. Watson interrupted. "They say an army travels on its stomach. What do you say, General Scherman?"

"I say, let's eat." Bob Scherman grinned. "Eat first, then talk. Squat, boys, squat."

Hastily the boys scrambled for places around the long table which, on other days of the week, served as Mr. Watson's work bench. Lined up on the

shelves along the whitewashed walls were signs of
past Cub activities, the rope machine which Andy
had started for one of his Lion achievements, the
exhibit of knots which had won first prize at a Pack
meeting last year, Bob's model planes. Sam's but-
terfly collection, regularly dusted off when the
Huntsville Hardware Store displayed Cub work during Boy Scout Week, hung from a nail under the
window. An American flag and the Den banner
were neatly furled in the far corner of the room.

Perched on up-ended packing boxes, the boys
waited while Chuck poured the orange soda and
Bob counted out doughnuts, two for each. For a
while the only sounds came from the gulping of
pop and the movement of jaws up and down on the
sugary doughnuts.

When he had wiped the last crumb from his
mouth with the back of his hand, Chuck announced, "Okay, boys. The meeting will come to
order."

Chuck's announcement brought on a flurry of
activity. Andy went off to hunt for the dues box
while Bob read the roll call. "Chuck Watson,

Jamie Lee, Pete Gold, Tim Brady, Jack Bell, Andy Hobbs, Sam Roth. And me. All present or accounted for," he sang out.

When Andy returned with the cardboard shoebox labeled "DUE" in big red letters, each boy fished a nickel from his pocket and carefully deposited it in the slot cut in the top of the box. "Now the flag ceremony," Mrs. Watson reminded them.

Jamie ran to the corner of the room. "My turn today," he said importantly. "I hold the flag." Although the boys lined up and solemnly pledged allegiance it was clear that their thoughts were wandering elsewhere. When Mrs. Watson prompted them on the Cub Scout promise they were in a hurry to be finished. "Ipromisedomybestbesquareobeylawofthepack" rang out in a hasty chorus, with Jamie's thin voice several words behind the rest.

"Now let's get down to business," Chuck suggested.

Grouping their packing boxes around Mrs. Watson, the boys listened quietly as she explained the Pack project. "At four o'clock we're going in to see

Mr. Cheyney, the editor of *The Enterprise*. His grandfather founded the paper in 1851, when Huntsville was just a fishing village on the Sound. This afternoon he's going to show us around his office and answer our questions. If we want to, we can go back later in the week and see them actually at work on the paper."

"But I don't see——" "But how can we——" "But——" eight voices started at once.

"How can you do an exciting report on a newspaper?" Mrs. Watson smiled. "Well, why don't we give it a try? It might turn out to be more exciting than you think."

"Oh, pooh." Chuck was disgusted.

"No," Andy said seriously, "I've been thinking. Lots of things happen on newspapers. Haven't you seen it in the movies?"

"Yeah, like what?" Bob wanted to know.

"Oh, scoops and reporters solving mysteries and finding lost people and—and—lots of things," Andy finished lamely.

"Andy's right," Sam defended his friend. "I saw a neat movie about a reporter once. Besides, we're

25

stuck with this. We have to show Mr. Thompson and those other kids. I move we take a vote."

"Vote?" Bob questioned. "What in heck are we going to vote about?"

"I vote that we decide to bring in the best report on Know Your Neighborhood," Sam solemnly proposed.

"Best and most exciting," Andy added. "All in favor say 'AYE.' "

After eight shouted "AYES," the boys grabbed caps and jackets from the pegs at the basement door while Mrs. Watson went around to the garage for her car. Promptly at four she parked in front of *The Enterprise* office and the Blackhawk Braves tumbled out. It looked a little like that act in the circus when dozens of clowns and midgets pour out of a broken-down automobile.

Mr. Cheyney was waiting at the door to greet them. "Hello, Mrs. Watson. Hello, Chuck," he smiled. "Will you introduce me to your friends?"

After he had shaken hands with each boy, he led them through a little wooden gate into a room filled with battered desks and typewriters. One whole wall was taken up by a bookcase. Sam, edging over to look at the books, saw that they were all the same, black leather, with *The Huntsville Enterprise* stamped on in gold. Each one had a different date, starting with 1851, in the far corner of the top shelf. Right in front of Sam were the ones from the 1860s. It would be fun to read about the Civil War in a newspaper written right during the fighting, he thought. He nudged Bob, who was always saying that General Sherman was the best general in the war. But Bob was listening to Mr. Cheyney and just shook his head at Sam.

"I wonder what the fellows would like to hear about first," Mr. Cheyney asked Mrs. Watson.

"The boys don't think there's any excitement at a newspaper office," she explained. "What can you offer them?"

Mr. Cheyney thought a minute. "We have some surprising things around here. Pigs and slugs, for instance. And there's always pie and gingerbread. We used to have a devil too, but he went away to college."

The boys were mystified. This wasn't at all what

27

they had expected to find. Shyly Jamie raised his hand. "I'd like some pie," he suggested. "I don't like gingerbread much."

Mr. Cheyney's eyes twinkled behind his glasses. "Well, come right this way, son. Most of the interesting things are in the pressroom."

Following him, the boys walked into a long barn-like room, three or four times the size of the outer

office. As big as a bowling alley, Chuck thought. On one side were two tall machines with a series of bells and pulleys and rollers, and a keyboard that looked like a typewriter. On the other was a row of waist-high, stone-topped tables. The floor was littered with silvery-gray metal shavings. The printing press, longer than an automobile, stretched across the back of the room. Wherever they stood there was a strange smell, different from anything they had ever smelled before.

But for the moment the boys were not interested in new smells. They were looking along the table tops and the shelves stacked high with paper for something familiar, for some signs of the pie Mr. Cheyney had talked about. All except Sam. He was looking for pigs and slugs.

Mr. Cheyney let them wander around for a moment. Then he led them to one of the tables and picked up a piece of metal. It had letters standing out on it, but they were upside down. "Tʜᴇ ᴊᴇꜱᴘʀɪᴛᴇ" it seemed to say. "Here, son." He handed it to Jamie. "Here's your pie."

Mr. Cheyney and Mrs. Watson couldn't help

laughing at the disappointed expression on Jamie's face. "That was a printer's joke. It just goes to show you, there's all kinds of pie in this world," Mr. Cheyney chuckled.

"When a piece of type is jumbled we call it 'pi' or 'pied.' It's spelled p-i, though, not p-i-e, like apple pie. You see"—he took the type back from Jamie—"these letters are upside down, but if they were printed on paper they would read 'The Etrrpsei' instead of 'The Enterprise.'"

"I suppose the gingerbread is like that too?" Chuck suggested.

"Another pressroom joke," Mr. Cheyney said. "Gingerbread is what printers call the lines and curlicues you see around the borders of advertisements." He pointed out some "gingerbread" in a newspaper on the table.

"Then the pigs and slugs aren't real either?" Sam was only a little disappointed. All along he had suspected some kind of a catch to Mr. Cheyney's story.

"Well, they're real enough," Mr. Cheyney replied, "but they aren't alive. They're made of lead.

Here." He picked up a metal bar, the same color as the shavings on the floor. Passing it to Sam, he warned, "Watch out, it's heavy. That's a pig."

Sam held it carefully. "Weighs about ten pounds," he guessed.

"Right," Mr. Cheyney agreed. "This little pig is the metal from which the type is cast. It's melted into liquid in those linotype machines." The boys moved to the tall machines near the door. "The linotyper pushes down the letters on the keyboard, just the way you'd work a typewriter," Mr. Cheyney continued, "and the molten metal pours into type molds, depending on which key is pushed. When he's written a whole line of letters they drop out on this little shelf. A line of type is called a slug. It's still warm when it comes out of the machine."

Chuck gingerly fingered one of the lead pieces. "Go on, take one," the editor said. "This kind of slug won't bite."

"No kind of slug bites," Sam muttered to Andy.

But Mr. Cheyney didn't hear him. He was giving each boy a line of type and showing him how to ink it with one of the rollers lying on the stone-topped table. "Now proof it up," he suggested.

"What's that?" Jamie asked.

"Press it down on this paper," Mr. Cheyney explained. "You can read it then."

"Hey, mine says 'Continued on page 3,' " Chuck discovered.

"Beat you," Bob called. "Mine's 'Continued on page 7.' "

"Mine's different," Jamie announced with some pride. "Mine says 'Fair and warmer today.' This is just like my printing set at home," he told Mr. Cheyney, "but my type is rubber."

After each boy had tried out his slug to discover what the upside-down letters said when they were printed, Mr. Cheyney led them back to the press. His eyes twinkled again. "I forgot to tell you that we have a lockup man and a bed, and one man who's in charge of killing."

This time the boys knew he was joking and nobody would bite. Not even Jamie.

"Can't fool you any more, can I?" The editor smiled. "The lockup man puts together the type for all the stories that are going on one page and locks it into an iron frame. When he has two pages locked up, he puts them on the bed of the press."

Peering into the big press, the boys saw where the type was placed and the rollers which automatically inked it. The ink was heavy and black, thicker than maple syrup. It didn't smell like maple syrup, though. It was the ink which the boys had smelled when they first came into the room. Near the press the smell was strong and it made them clear their throats and cough a little.

"But you haven't told us about the killer," Jamie reminded Mr. Cheyney. The other boys looked embarrassed. Each of them had privately determined not to ask any more dumb questions.

As if he understood their feelings, Mr. Cheyncy didn't tease Jamie. Instead, he explained that after they had printed all the copies of the paper that were needed, they took the type out of the forms and melted it so they could use the same lead over again. "That's what we call killing the type," he said. "Come on down to the basement and I'll show you how it's done."

In the cluttered cellar a big iron pot filled with

silvery liquid was swinging from an old-fashioned stove. "The slugs are melted in this pot," he explained. He ladled some of the liquid into a long mold lying on the floor. "When that's cool it will be one of the pigs that Sam, here, was interested in."

As they followed the editor up the narrow basement stairs, the boys were quiet. The pressroom had been better than they had expected, and Mr. Cheyney was swell. They liked his jokes about pi and pigs and the way he used words like "press run" and "linotype" as if they were old hands at the newspaper business. I'd like to come back and see those machines when they're working, Chuck told himself. But, each boy was thinking, what kind of report can we do on *The Enterprise* that will make Den One sit up and take notice?

Leading them into the front office, Mr. Cheyney invited them to try out the swivel chairs while he perched on the corner of a desk. "Let's have some questions," he suggested.

There was a long pause. Then Bob asked about the devil who'd gone to college.

"Oh, I'd forgotten about him," Mr. Cheyney smiled. "Printer's devil is an old name for a youngster who works in a print shop, sort of an errand boy, who wants to learn the trade. Ben Franklin was a printer's devil. Between the Army and college, I can't keep one these days."

"I'd like to be a printer's devil," Jamie, who could never keep quiet for very long, announced.

"All right, son." Mr. Cheyney's face was serious. "Come around to see me when you've had a few more years of school and we'll talk business."

"How about how you get your news?" Andy wanted to know. "Do you just walk around looking for things to happen, or do people telephone or what?"

"Good question," Mr. Cheyney said. "And the answer is, a little of both. Tom Burt—guess you boys know him—covers the police station. He's down there most of the day, so if your dog bites Chuck, or if Jamie's father gets a ticket for speeding, we know about it as soon as the desk sergeant does. I take care of the City Council and School Board meetings and Mrs. Rowe, our society re-

36

porter, goes to the Newcomers' Club and Ladies' Aid luncheons. Mostly when people get married or have babies they call to tell her about it. We also have correspondents in Greensboro and Riverton who telephone or write when anything happens in their neighborhood.

"Seems as if the people in Huntsville are more interested in fires than anything else," he continued. "See that box on the wall? It's hooked up with the alarm at the firehouse and——"

As the boys stared, the clapper attached to the box Mr. Cheyney was pointing to began to beat a desperate tattoo. One-two-three. One-two. One-two-three. One-two.

"Three long, two short," Mr. Cheyney translated. "Fire's over at the shore. In a minute the engine will pass by here."

At the sound of the fire siren, eight Blackhawk Braves spun out of their swivel chairs and scrambled to the big plate-glass window at the front of the office. Sure enough, there came the hook-and-ladder truck. Waving happily from the front seat were familiar blue-capped faces from Den One.

37

Chief Whelan's red coupé followed the truck as it clanged up the hill. Johnny Adams and Tom Stein, heads erect and eyes shining, were riding proudly beside the chief.

A loud sigh escaped from eight throats in *The Enterprise* office. "Den One," somebody said in a strangled voice. "Those guys." "Betcha it's a false alarm."

As the last sound of the siren died away, the boys listlessly turned from the window. "Well, it can't be *much* of a fire," Mr. Cheyney tried to comfort them. "Only one alarm."

But words, no matter how well meant, couldn't satisfy Den Two. Eight pairs of legs swung from the swivel chairs, keeping time with the pendulum of the big wooden clock on the wall. Eight pairs of eyes moodily studied the floor. For the first time in their lives, the Blackhawk Braves had nothing to say.

3 _EXCITEMENT AT THE ENTERPRISE_

Mr. Cheyney cleared his throat twice and Mrs. Watson looked at the boys in a frowning sort of way. Finally Andy lifted his head. "Doesn't anything exciting happen around here?" he asked.

"Exciting?" Mr. Cheyney thought about the question. "Well now, just what did you have in mind?"

"Oh, like finding lost people or solving crimes or murders—not killing type." Andy's voice was almost rude.

The corners of Mr. Cheyney's mouth turned up a little. "This is a pretty quiet town," he reminded them. "Oh, on Saturday nights a few people get into mischief sometimes, but except for that hit-and-run driver last year, Chief Rockey hasn't had a long-term boarder in his jail for—let's see—must be ten years. Hasn't been a really serious crime committed in this town since that bank robbery back in the thirties."

"That's an awfully long time ago," Jamie sighed. The other boys continued their study of the floor.

Mr. Cheyney nodded. "Yes, that was before any of you were born. Back in"—he thought a moment—"1938. Didn't any of you hear about it?"

The boys silently shook their heads.

"It was right across the street at the Huntsville National Bank." Now Mr. Cheyney was trying hard to interest them. "Jim Odell was teller then. He looked through his little window and saw a masked man pointing a gun at him. 'Hand me all the money you've got,' the man said. There wasn't anything for Jim to do but obey. Then the robber

40

locked Jim up and walked out. The whole thing didn't take five minutes."

"But did they catch him?" "How much money did he get?" "Did he leave any fingerprints?" The boys were finding their voices.

"Whoa, wait a minute, one at a time." Mr. Cheyney held up his hand to slow down the questions. "He took about five thousand dollars. No, they never found him or his fingerprints either."

"But what did you do?" Even Chuck sounded hopeful now. "Did you hunt for him? Did you look for clues?"

"First thing we did was put out an extra—a special edition of the paper," Mr. Cheyney explained. "First extra *The Enterprise* printed since the day Lincoln was assassinated. We didn't look for clues, because that was a job for the police. They had special deputies watching every train and bus leaving Huntsville, and they sent out a four-state alarm, wiring as much of a description of the robber as Jim could give. Every bank in the country had a list of the numbers of the stolen bills and we printed the list too, so the stores here could watch for them.

Funny thing, not a single one of those bills ever turned up at any bank."

"Well, maybe he spent the money," Jamie's eyes were growing rounder. "Maybe he spent the money instead of putting it in his bank account."

The swivel chairs squeaked in chorus. Everyone, at the same moment, tried to straighten out Jamie about money and stores and banks. Pete, whose father owned the Sweet Shop, impatiently informed him that storekeepers took the money that people paid them and brought it to the bank each week.

"That's right," Mr. Cheyney summed up the discussion. "I'm afraid that all money starts out in banks and ends up in banks."

"How well I know it." Mrs. Watson sighed.

The boys flopped back in their chairs again. This was beginning to sound like grownups' talk and the echo of the fire siren was still ringing in their ears. They wanted something—anything—to happen.

"Would you like to see the stories we wrote about the robbery?" Mr. Cheyney cheerfully offered.

The boys nodded politely, but without any great

show of interest. Andy and Chuck walked to the bookshelves and helped Mr. Cheyney lift out two of the big leatherbound back issues of *The Enterprise*. Lugging them to the long table near the window, they dropped them with a resounding thud.

Mr. Cheyney picked up one of the books and blew off a cloud of dust. "I think this is the right volume. It was just after Labor Day, I remember. Yep, here it is." Flattening out the pages, he began to read.

" 'The Huntsville National Bank was robbed of $5,210 two hours ago when a masked man approached the teller's window, waved a gun at Teller James Odell and ordered him to "hand over the cash." Mr. Odell, who was preparing a pay roll for the B. G. Nut and Bolt Company, Whitehill Road, slid the bills along the counter. "Now put up your hands," the masked man ordered.' "

Mr. Cheyney paused to clear his throat and the boys moved in closer. Jamie was small enough to duck under Mr. Cheyney's arm, where he could see the story for himself. Only Sam was squeezed

43

out of the half circle around the editor. He moved to the far side of the table and began to flip the pages of the other bound volume.

" 'As Mr. Odell backed away, his hands in the air, the robber counted the money. Apparently satisfied with the sum, he ordered the teller to give him one of the pay-roll boxes stacked at the far end of the counter. After dropping the money into the box, he backed Mr. Odell into the men's room, warned him to keep quiet, and locked him in.

" 'When Mrs. Robert James, 14 Maple Drive, came in to make her regular weekly deposit at 10:15, she heard Mr. Odell shouting and banging on the locked door. Quickly releasing him, she waited while he telephoned the police. Although Chief Rockey was on the scene of the robbery five minutes later, there was no trace of the masked man or his means of getaway.

" 'According to Mr. Odell, the robber was about five foot ten and weighed about 180 pounds. Because he wore a wide-brimmed hat and a mask over his eyes and nose, Mr. Odell could add little more to the description. The masked man wore

44

gloves, thus ruling out fingerprint clues to his identity.

" ' "This is the first robbery the Huntsville National Bank has ever had," Bank President Thomas Oakley said. "I have every confidence in Chief Rockey's ability to catch the man who did it." '

"That's the whole story from our extra edition," Mr. Cheyney said. "In the next issue we told about the work of the police and special deputies Chief Rockey swore in, and we printed the numbers of the missing bills."

Turning the pages of the old newspaper, he showed the boys the stories he was talking about. "Here"—he pointed—"is where Oakley offered a reward of one thousand dollars to anyone who turned in information leading to the arrest of the robber or the recovery of the money. I guess by that time he wasn't so sure that Rockey was going to get his man. We printed little articles about the search for another week or two and then we let the story die. There wasn't anything more to say about it."

"Wonder what did happen to the man?" Chuck thought out loud.

46

"And to the money," Andy added.

"I'd sure like to find it," Bob and Tim said at the same moment.

"So would a lot of other people," Mr. Cheyney agreed. Noticing Sam, who was still quietly reading his volume of *The Enterprise*, he tried to bring him into the conversation. "How about you, Sam? Wouldn't you like to find that money?"

Sam blinked at Mr. Cheyney. "What money? Oh, sure. Sure I'd like to find it. I was just reading a sort of interesting story," he explained apologetically. "About that drowned man Mr. Shipley found on the beach at Tod's Point. He had no iden"—he stumbled over the word—"no identification. Did they ever find out who he was?"

Mr. Cheyney turned Sam's paper around and looked at it for a moment. "No, I don't think they ever did. Of course, that happens every once in a while along the Sound here. Men falling off boats, maybe washed all the way over from the south shore. Sometimes they've been in the water for weeks and it's pretty hard to recognize them."

"But this wasn't just an ordinary fisherman or

sailor or anything," Sam insisted. "This man had no iden-identification on purpose. All the labels were cut out of his clothes and the police couldn't find a wallet or laundry marks or anything."

"So what?" Chuck wanted to know.

"Well, I think that's suspicious." Sam defended his story. "It happened just a couple of weeks after the bank robbery too."

Andy sat up suddenly. "What's it say about how he looked?"

Sam ran his fingers down the page of the newspaper. "Let's see. Five feet eight. One hundred and fifty pounds. Blond hair, blue eyes, no scars."

"Well, that's not much help," Bob pointed out. "That could be almost anybody. Your father looks like that, Chuck."

The boys were thoughtful for a moment. "You know," Andy slowly began, "like Mr. Cheyney says——"

Sam started to open his mouth. "Okay, Professor." Andy grinned at Sam. "As Mr. Cheyney says, Huntsville is a pretty quiet town. For years and years nothing happens. Then all of a sudden,

48

boom"—he banged his fist on the table—"there are two mysteries in two weeks. Maybe they're connected. Suppose this man was the robber."

"Oh, pooh." Chuck was more than doubtful. "It can't be the same guy. This drowned one was much smaller than the robber, for one thing."

"Just a sec. My father says——" Bob began. "He's a lawyer——" He turned to Mr. Cheyney. "My father says that witnesses never agree. That if two or three people see the same thing happen, they all tell about it differently. They've done tests about it—to prove it, I mean. It's psychology," he grandly explained.

"Pooh," Chuck repeated. "Betcha I can guess how much you weigh."

"Betcha can't. All of you boys guess," Bob suggested, "and we'll see how you come out."

"Eighty-two pounds," Chuck called out.

Andy studied Bob's chunky figure for a minute. "Seventy-two," he said.

"Well, what do the rest of you say?" Bob challenged them.

"Ninety." "Seventy-five." "Eighty-five," the

boys shouted. "Fifty-eight," Jamie chimed in last, naming his own weight.

"Wrong, wrong, wrong. You're all wrong." Bob was delighted. "I weigh exactly sixty-eight pounds with my shoes off. All of you were wrong and all of you guessed too much—except Jamie."

"Sure, don't you see." Sam's voice was growing hoarse the way it did when he was excited. "Mr. Odell, he was probably pretty scared when that man pointed the gun at him. The robber probably looked a lot taller and heavier to him than he really was. Because he was scared, I mean. That's psychology, too." He nodded to Bob.

Mrs. Watson, who had remained in her swivel chair in the corner of the room, now interrupted. "I imagine," she smiled, "that the police considered this when Mr. Shipley found the drowned man."

The boys turned to catch Mr. Cheyney's nod. "Now that you mention it, I believe they did think about your man. They had Odell look the body over, but he couldn't be sure one way or the other. The trouble was there was never anything actually linking the man to the robbery. He had no money in his pockets at all, not even a dime, as I remember. And it was the money the police were after."

When he paused, Mr. Cheyney found himself swamped with questions.

"But did they search where the body was found?"

"Weren't there any clues?"

"Did they check his fingerprints with the FBI?"

Laughing, the editor held up his hand again. "Just keep calm, boys, and I'll try to answer you all. I guess your Cubmaster should have assigned you to the police station. I never saw such a bunch of natural-born Dick Tracys. But I'll tell you one thing, fellows. There's no sense making a mystery where there isn't one. Chief Rockey checked the man's fingerprints and there was no record of them in Washington or anywhere. There was all kinds of wreckage washed up on the beach, but nothing that the police considered a clue. They couldn't prove that he wasn't the robber, but they certainly couldn't find anything that said that he was, either."

Andy, who had been looking through the old

newspapers, could hardly wait for Mr. Cheyney to finish. "But, look," he said. "They never found the money. Right? And the reason they never found it is because it was never spent. Right? That means that something must have happened to the man who stole it, and nobody else knew where it was hidden." Chuck looked as if he were about to interrupt, but Andy hurried on. "The bank was robbed on September eighth, and this man's body was found on September twenty-third. I think he must have had a hide-out some place along the Sound where he lived for those two weeks. I bet he figured that since the police were sending out alarms for him, the safest place to stay would be right in Huntsville."

"Well, but where's the money?" Jamie wanted to know.

"I vote we look for it. Jeepers, that would sure fix those Den One guys, if we found all that money." Andy's voice was dreamy.

"How could we find it now, after thirteen years?" Chuck snorted. "You crazy or something?"

Patiently Andy explained. "Since the robber

didn't expect to be drowned, he must have left the money in his hide-out or somewhere near it. All we have to do is find where he lived those two weeks and then look around there for the money. Smart brain," he added, tapping his own head so everyone would know whom he was talking about.

"All we have to do!" Bob groaned. "How in heck are we going to do that?"

Sam waved his hand wildly. "I know. I know. Right after school tomorrow we'll meet and divide up into teams and search all the land around Tod's Point. As soon as one of us finds a clue he'll give the Den whistle and we'll all get together and go to work on it."

"Oh no," Chuck howled. "Not tomorrow. Tomorrow's baseball practice. Besides, you won't find anything. Any clues the robber left would have been washed away long ago."

The boys turned from Chuck's disgusted face to Andy and Sam, who were bouncing up and down in excitement, then back to Chuck again. Baseball and common sense against robberies and rewards. It was a hard decision to make.

THE CUB SCOUT MYSTERY

Andy solved it for them. "You can play baseball any time," he reminded Chuck severely, "but it's like you said. The honor of the Blackhawk Braves is at stake."

That did it. With the rest of the boys plainly on his side, Andy turned to Mrs. Watson. In his most businesslike voice, he asked for permission to meet in her basement right after school tomorrow.

"Of course you can come," she agreed, "but honestly, boys, I think you've picked too tough a job for yourselves. It's certainly one way to know your neighborhood, but you mustn't be too disappointed if you don't find anything."

"Oh, don't worry about us," Andy assured her. "How about it, Chuck?"

Chuck shook his head. "I still think you're crazy, but I'll be there."

54

4 *THE TREASURE HUNT*

Three minutes after the bell rang out the end of another school day, each Blackhawk Brave was pedaling his bicycle in the direction of the Watsons'. While the rest of the boys let themselves in the basement door, Chuck went around to the kitchen to negotiate with his mother about refreshments. By the time he came down the stairs with a plateful of peanut-butter sandwiches, everyone was crowded around the table looking at a map which Andy had spread out.

55

"It's a Coast Guard map of this part of the Sound," he explained to Chuck. "It shows all the inlets and buoys and reefs and stuff. U. S. Coast and Geodetic Survey." He proudly traced the letters in the upper left-hand corner.

But Chuck was not to be won over by big words. "Does it show where the bank money is buried?" he asked as he plunked down the sandwiches.

"Yeah." Bob supported him between mouthfuls. "How are we going to work this, anyway?"

Andy took three thoughtful bites of his sandwich, using the tip of his tongue to dislodge some peanut butter which stuck to the roof of his mouth. "Well, this is the way I figure it. We divide up into four teams. Say Chuck and Bob, Pete and Jamie, Tim and Jack, and Sam and me." The boys nodded agreement. "Then each team takes a territory, starting at Tod's Point and going down to about"—he consulted the map—"Tappan's Landing."

"Dibs on Tod's Point," Chuck called out.

"Why go all the way to Tappan's Landing?" Bob asked. "The man was found at Tod's Point."

Andy smiled in a superior way, ignoring Bob's

question. "Okay, Chuck and Bob, Tod's Point down to that big rock where we played King on the Mountain. Pete and Jamie, you take from there to the town beach." He drew a line on the map with his stubby forefinger.

"Tim and Jack from the beach to the McIntyre estate. You know, where they have that dock with the diving boards?" Tim and Jack nodded their understanding. "And Sam and I will cover from there to Tappan's Landing. Let's meet here tomorrow, same time, to tell what we found."

"*If* we find anything," Chuck insisted.

Anxious to put off an argument, Pete suggested a vote. "All in favor say 'Aye.'"

After hearty "Ayes," the boys picked up their jackets. Andy carefully folded the map and stuffed it in his hip pocket. Last to slam the cellar door, he wheeled out his bike while Sam looked questioningly at him.

"I know what you're going to say," Andy challenged. "Why did I let Chuck and the others have the territory where the body was found? Currents, my good man, currents. Here, let me show you."

Pushing the kick-stand on his bike so that it would stand in the driveway, Andy took out the map again. "You know how the undertow carries you along when you're swimming at the beach? Well, the way this map shows, the currents around here carry you north and west. Of course, the direction of the wind makes a difference too, but I figure that if the man's body was found at Tod's Point, he must have fallen in the water some place south and east of there. Like Tappan's Landing, maybe."

Sam looked from the map to Andy's excited face. "Smart brain," he said admiringly.

"Smart brain," Andy agreed. "Once when Dad and I were rowing, we lost an oar. We didn't find it till the next day, way up the beach," he explained in a more modest tone.

The two boys pedaled along Shore Road to the McIntyre estate, coasting down the wide gravel driveway to the shore. Leaving their bikes at the edge of the dock, they stopped to look around. From the McIntyres' house at the top of the hill, smooth lawns stretched to the water front. Beyond the small sandy area which surrounded the dock, thick marsh grass, bent flat by the wind, grew to the water's edge. In the distance was Tappan's Landing, a breakwater of rocks, all that was left of an old sea wall. As far as they could see marsh grass and inlets of sea water alternated with triangles of coarse sand.

Turning south, the boys tramped along in silence, the only sounds the squeak of their sneakers on the slippery grass and the crying of the gulls circling and dipping overhead. Occasionally Sam stooped to pick up a shell, pocketing the likely specimens and tossing the broken ones toward the water. Once he found a cluster of mussels all covered with barnacles, and held it up for Andy to see. Wordlessly, Andy brushed it away. He had more important things to consider.

"It's like a treasure hunt," Sam finally ventured. "Soon as we find the first clue, we'll know where to go next."

"Only, in a treasure hunt Mrs. Watson or our mothers know where the clues are and where they've hidden the treasure. This is harder." Andy sounded worried.

Again there was silence. Sam, a few feet ahead

59

of Andy, kicked at something heavy in the grass. "Hey," he called in sudden excitement. "Hey, look at this here, Andy."

With heart beating fast, Andy took a long step over a pool of water, slipped, and landed with one foot in the pool. Shaking off his wet sneaker, he hurried to Sam's side. Sam was kneeling beside a leather-brown, shield-shaped creature with a sharp, pointed tail. As they watched, the animal slowly dug itself into the sand.

When it was no longer visible, Andy exploded. "Gosh darn it, Sam! That's no clue. That's nothing but a horseshoe crab. And I'm soaking wet."

"Nothing but a horseshoe crab?" Sam's voice hoarsened. "*Nothing but a horseshoe crab?* Andrew Hobbs, that's the biggest horseshoe crab I ever saw. Bet it was two feet long. I'm sorry about your sneaker, though. Let's sit down a minute and try to dry you off."

Andy picked out a rock to sit on and unlaced his sneaker while Sam fished a smudged handkerchief from his pocket. Accepting it with a nod, Andy took off his dripping sock and vigorously rubbed his foot.

"Sam," he said thoughtfully, "we've got to figure this out. There's no point in just walking around. Where would you go if you were a robber and had to hide out here for a few weeks?"

Sam, fingering a piece of seaweed, thought for a moment. After he had made the seaweed pop, he looked up with a gleam in his eye. "Beach cottage," he said. "There are three of them right along here."

"But there would be people living there," Andy pointed out.

"Nope. It was after Labor Day. Everybody always goes back to the city the day before Labor Day to miss the crowds on the roads."

"We-l-l-l——" Andy was still doubtful. "Those cottages have had so many different people living in them since then that I don't know what clues we'd find. But let's go down and look around. Maybe we'll get some ideas."

Stuffing his wet sock into his pocket, he pulled on his equally wet sneaker and stood up. Sam, dusting off the seat of his pants, took a last longing look at the spot where the horseshoe crab had buried itself. Now that they had a plan again, both

61

boys felt more cheerful and ready for anything.

Around a curve in the beach the boys spotted the wooden stairway which led up the hill to the cottages. "Beat you to the stairs!" Andy suddenly shouted. "Last one there is a rotten egg."

Both boys dashed ahead, slipping and sliding on the wet grass. Andy was first to touch the stair post, Sam a breathless second. Panting as they climbed the long flight, they looked up at the three cottages, perched side by side. Bide-a-Wee, By-the-Sea, and Saltair, neat little signs in front proclaimed them.

Bide-a-Wee and By-the-Sea were exactly alike— white clapboard, red roof, and tiny screened porch. Saltair was larger, with an extra wing on the south side and a lawn big enough for a drooping mulberry tree. All three were owned by Phil Simms, proprietor of the Huntsville Lumber Yard. He had built them himself, and from the fifteenth of June until Labor Day, they were overflowing with parents, children, and dogs.

Andy and Sam tried the screen door on Bide-a-Wee, and finding that it swung open, cautiously walked in. "Mrs. Simms must have started cleaning up already for the summer people," Sam noted. "Usually these doors are locked tight."

It took only a few minutes for the boys to go through the bare rooms of Bide-a-wee and By-the-Sea and the slightly more spacious quarters of Salt-air, which boasted a bathtub as well as a shower, and a rag rug on the living-room floor.

"Doesn't give me any ideas," Andy said, "but let's look around the back."

Each cottage had its own tiny garden, the flower beds carefully enclosed with a border of clam shells. A path led back to the garage and the road. "Of course"—Sam thought out loud as he turned over one of the shells—"he might have buried the money here. Maybe these shells are supposed to point to the spot."

The boys considered the garden design carefully. Each row of shells started at the front of the house and curved around to the back stoop. Dozens of houses in Huntsville had gardens laid out exactly like these.

"Nope," Andy finally decided. "Mrs. Simms fixed those to look like the ones on Shore Road.

63

he wasn't arguing any more. "I don't know. But he never mentioned a boat. I wonder now."

As he slowly dragged out the last words, Andy slid his map from his pocket. Flattening it out on his knee, he searched for Gull Island. "You've guessed it!" he shouted. "They waded. He waded. Oh boy, Sam, I'm sure we got it."

"Have it," Sam couldn't stop himself from saying. "What, Andy, what? Stop hopping up and down and tell me who you're talking about."

"My father. I mean the robber. He waded out to Gull Island. Look." Andy calmed down enough to show Sam the map. At "mean low tide," the map said, there was a row of rocks running from Tappan's Landing to Gull Island.

"I still don't get it," Sam mourned. "I see the rocks on the map all right, but they aren't there. I mean, look for yourself." He pointed to the unbroken stretch of water which separated them from the island.

"Look, you dope!" Andy was breathless now. "The tide is coming in, right?" Sam nodded. "Well, when the tide is low some of those rocks are out of the water and the rest are just a little way under. It should be a cinch to wade out there."

Wordlessly, the boys scrambled down the stairs and ran to the end of the breakwater. Sure enough, if they looked carefully they could see the rocks under water, stretching out into the Sound. Andy sat down and started unlacing his sneakers.

"This is crazy," Sam protested. "It'll be dark in an hour and the tide is coming in, you said. Let's come back tomorow at low tide."

68

"Okay," Andy agreed, "but right after school tomorrow. I got to get to that shack."

"Have to——"

"Okay, I have to get up to that shack," Andy interrupted. "Race you up the beach."

With eyes shining and hair blowing in the wind, both boys ran along the shore. This time it was Sam who slipped and fell in a hidden pool and got up with his sneakers covered with salt water and seaweed. Andy grasped his elbow while Sam hopped first on one foot and then the other in a hopeless effort to dry them. "Boy, will I catch Hail Columbia if my mother sees these."

"Go in the side door," Andy wisely advised. "Besides, it's in a good cause."

The sun was sinking behind the trees as they pedaled home. By the time they reached Midland Road, where Sam turned left up the hill and Andy right, it was almost dark and passing cars were switching on their lights.

"So long, pal." Sam waved as he turned his handle bars.

"So long— partner," Andy shouted after him.

5   *THE OLD CARRIAGE ROAD*

With his bike stowed in the garage, Andy followed his own advice and quietly let himself in the side door. "Hi, Mom," he called as he changed his wet shoes. After thoughtfully washing his face and brushing back his hair, he walked to the kitchen.

"Hello, dear." His mother smiled at him. "What have you been up to?"

"Oh, nothing much. Cub project. Know Your Neighborhood." Andy side-stepped in front of the stove, lifting pot lids and sniffing hungrily. "When'll Dad be home?"

His mother rapped his knuckles lightly. "Keep out of my supper," she ordered. "Dad will be home at 6:30."

"What did you think, stupe?" his sister asked. "Dad always comes home at 6:30, winter or summer, rain or shine or snow." Sally, four years older than Andy, was sitting at the far end of the kitchen counter filing her nails. Andy glared at her and she glared back at him.

"Mom, can I have something to eat? I'm starved." Andy pulled open the cupboard door, searching for a cracker.

Again his mother rapped his knuckles. "Supper's almost ready and you're not going to have a mouthful until Dad gets in. Sit down and tell me what you did today."

"Always hungry," Sally muttered. "Disgusting."

Andy opened his mouth to answer her, then had a better idea. Instead, he started to sing

"I've got a mule. Her name is Sal.
Fifteen years on the Erie Canal.
She's a good old worker and a good old pal——"

71

"Make him stop, Mother," Sally groaned.

"That's just a song we learned in school, in music class," Andy defended himself. But he had more important things to do than to tease Sally. "Mom, do you think Dad knows about tides?"

His mother was stirring the gravy. "What about tides?" she asked. "What are you up to? This is no time of the year to be playing around the shore."

"Oh, we're just collecting stuff for our report on Know Your Neighborhood, and I'm supposed to find out about Huntsville tides," Andy carefully explained. "High, low—stuff like that."

"I don't know much about tides, but even I know enough to look in *The Enterprise* to see when they're going to be high and low." Mrs. Hobbs smiled.

"Where's the paper?" Andy looked around the kitchen.

"At the front door, stupe." His sister pointed in that direction. "Where did you think it would be?"

Grumblingly wondering why she never brought the paper in, Andy rushed down the hall to the door. Back in the kitchen, he scanned *The Enter-*

prise's front page. From her station at the stove, his mother pointed to the box which told about the weather.

"Fair and warmer tomorrow," he read out loud. "Moderate to fresh southwesterly winds. High tide, 9:31 A.M. Low tide, 3:47 P.M. Oh boy, that does it."

Scarcely hearing Sally's "What does what?" Andy folded the paper and carried it to the living room. He was thinking so hard that he stumbled over the footstool in front of Dad's big chair and landed in the chair face down. Righting himself, he laid the paper on the little table where Dad liked to find it after supper. Still lost in thought, he poked the footstool with the toe of his shoe until he could slump down and rest his feet on it.

Three forty-seven meant that he and Sam could go to the beach after school and walk right out to Gull Island. They would have to call off the meeting of the Den. Or would it be better to round up the whole gang and go out to the island together? Andy lifted his head a minute, then dropped back on the soft cushions. Nope, this was a job for Sam and himself. They could let the others in on it after they had it all figured out.

His father's cheery "Hello" from the front door interrupted his planning. Jumping up, Andy took his topcoat and hung it up in the closet.

"Why, thanks, Andy." His father sounded surprised. "What have you been up to? Had a good day?"

Andy nodded, then rushed to the dining room as Sally called, "Come and get it!"

"Sally," his mother scolded as he pulled out his chair, "I wish you'd stop that silly 'Come and get it.' Why can't you just say, 'Dinner's ready'?"

"Aw, she heard that in a movie. She'll outgrow it." Andy was in a peace-making mood. Besides, he was hungry.

While he went to work on the pot roast and mashed potatoes, Mother and Dad and Sally talked about the high school debating club and the way beef had gone up another four cents. By the time he had flattened out his third portion of potatoes and ladled gravy into the hollow, Andy felt ready to talk again.

"Say, Dad." He kept his voice casual. "You haven't told us in a long time about how you used to play pirates out on Gull Island."

Dad looked surprised. "Well, no. Seems as if pirates is an old-fashioned game. All you kids want is cowboys and Indians and bang-bang-bang." Dad pointed his forefinger at Andy as if he were shooting him.

"Cowboys and Indians," Andy groaned. "That's for little kids."

"What do you want to know about Gull Island?" Dad asked.

"Well, Sam and I were walking along the shore today—it's for the Cub project." Andy hastily turned to his mother. "And we were looking at the island. I told him about when you were a boy. We wondered how you ever got out there. Unless you swam, that is."

"No, we didn't swim out." His father shook his head. "There used to be an old carriage road that led out to the island. A long time ago that was all part of the Kirby estate. The Kirbys used to own all that water-front land, the hill where the

Simmses' cottages are and clear out to the main road. Their house burned down when I was about your age. Biggest fire Huntsville ever had."

Andy knew all about the Kirby fire, It was one of his father's favorite stories. Anxiously, he tried to bring the discussion back to the business at hand. "But what about the road?" he reminded his father.

"The road? Oh yes." Dad nodded. "The road was built when the Kirbys first settled here. It was made of huge flat rocks, each one four or five feet across. They sank posts along both sides, sort of bulkheads, to keep the water from shifting the rocks during winter storms. Don't know how they ever managed to build it, without modern equipment. It was quite an engineering stunt. You see, the Misses Kirby liked to bathe from Gull Island."

"They called it bathing in those days, not swimming," his mother interrupted. "My father used to tell me how Miss Amanda and Miss Priscilla Kirby drove out to the island in a carriage pulled by two horses."

"Our pirates' den was really their old bath-
76

house." Dad picked up the story. "In the summer —we didn't have camps in those days like you have—we'd go out there every week end and cook our meals on the big outdoor fireplace they'd built."

"Yes, but what happened to the road?" Andy was getting impatient.

"After all the Kirbys died or moved away and they broke up the estate no one ever kept up the road," Dad explained. "Most of the posts were gone when I was a boy and there were places where we had to jump over two- and three-foot gaps. But it was the big hurricane that finally washed it out."

"Hurricane?" Sally was interested now. There had been a storm last fall which had blown down all the wires and left the Hobbses without electricity or telephone service for two days. "When was it? Was it worse than the one we had this year?"

"Oh, much worse," Dad assured her. "It must have been about 1939 or 1940."

"No"—Mother was positive—"Sally was just a

baby, and you, Andy, weren't even born yet. The hurricane was in 1938."

"Nineteen thirty-eight?" Andy forgot about speaking quietly at the dinner table. He positively shouted. "When was the hurricane?"

"Nineteen thirty-eight, you dope." Sally had remembered to be superior again.

Ignoring her, Andy turned to his father. "No, no. I mean what month?"

"It was September," his mother said. "I remember it was September because it was just after Labor Day."

When he heard "Labor Day," Andy hopped up and down in his chair. "September, Labor Day, oh boy!" was all he could say for a minute. Quieting down with obvious effort, he appealed to his mother to remember the exact day. His face fell when she shook her head.

"Listen, Andy, what's this all about?" Dad wanted to know. "I don't know the day, but if you'll get me the World Almanac after you've helped Mother clear the table, we can look it up. But why are you so excited about the date?"

Andy rose and started carrying dishes toward the kitchen. Over his shoulder, when Dad couldn't see his face, he called, "Cub project. It's a secret now so I can't tell you about it."

"Cub's honor?" His father smiled.

"Sort of," Andy agreed. The honor of the Blackhawk Braves, anyway, he told himself.

In the kitchen Sally reminded him that it was his turn to dry the silver. He started to argue with her, but thought better of it. No sense letting everyone see how excited he was. Tumbling the silver into the drawer in double-quick time, he raced for the bookcase in the living room.

"What's it look like, Dad?" he asked.

"What's what?" Dad looked up from *The Enterprise.* "Oh, the World Almanac. It's got a red cover. I think I see it over there on the bottom shelf, next to the encyclopedia."

Following Dad's pointing finger, Andy pulled out the almanac and carried it to Dad's chair. With heads bumping, they looked through the index. "Hurricanes, Descriptive," his father mumbled. "Disasters, see Disasters, page 305. Yes, here it is."

Andy stood very close to the chair while his father read, " 'High winds swept the Atlantic Coast from the Carolinas to Maine. Thousands were made homeless and property valued at $40,000,000 destroyed. September 21.' "

Andy could scarcely keep from shouting again as he returned the book to its place on the shelf. September twenty-first. Everything fitted. The robbery, September eighth. Road washed out, September twenty-first. Robber's body found September

80

twenty-third. Forty million dollars worth of property destroyed, including the old carriage road. For a moment he thought of calling Sam to tell him the good news. But the phone was in the dining room and Sally was sure to listen and ask questions. Better to wait until he saw him at school in the morning.

School made him think of homework, which was still untouched. Although he felt as if he were walking in a dream, a cops-and-robbers dream, he made his way to his desk and slowly copied his spelling words and did his arithmetic. Tonight he wasn't going to tease to stay up late and listen to the radio. He wanted to get into bed with the light out so he could think without being interrupted.

Surprised to find Andy in his room without his usual argument, Mrs. Hobbs came in and sat on his bed for a good night talk. "Listen, Son," she warned him. "I don't know what you're up to and I suppose it's all right, but I don't want you and Sam fooling around the beach. It's not warm enough yet for wet feet and I hate to think what would happen if you slipped on those rocks and fell in. There's just nobody around within calling distance at this time of the year."

"Don't worry, Mom," Andy reassured her. "We'll be all right." He felt a little guilty after she kissed him good night. At least I didn't promise anything, he comforted himself.

6

Andy was out of the house so quickly the next morning that he forgot his lunch and had to go back for it. "Haste makes waste," Sally smiled sweetly at him when he grabbed it from the kitchen table. As he ran, two steps at a time, from the porch to his bicycle, he thought for a moment about sisters and how they always thought they were so smart. Just wait, he promised himself, I'll fix her one of these days.

Pedaling his bike up the hill, he resolutely put

83

Sally from his mind. The important thing was to catch Sam before school started so that he could tell him about the hurricane and all he'd found out. Fortunately, Sam was just parking his bike in the bike rack when Andy reached the schoolyard. There was time for a quick conference before the bell called them to class.

School dragged endlessly that morning. In arithmetic, they were reviewing fractions, and although Andy added the same figures three times they still looked wrong. He was beginning to wear a hole in his paper with his eraser but the fourth time he copied the fractions they were right. Dumb brain, he scolded himself.

Finally, the lunch bell buzzed. As the class was lining up to walk to the cafeteria, Andy and Sam moved up and down the line, giving the Cub handshake to the members of Den Two. In the language of the Blackhawk Braves this meant, "Let's get together for a pow-wow."

While the rest of the fourth and fifth grades stormed the cafeteria counters, Den Two assembled just inside the door for a quick confer-

84

ence. "What did you find?" everyone chorused.

Andy smiled mysteriously. "I can't tell you now. But Sam and I have a—a——"

"A theory," Sam supplied the word.

"A theory that we want to work on today," Andy continued. "Let's call off the meeting this afternoon and get together at the Watsons' tomorrow. Did any of the rest of you find anything?"

Shaking their heads, the other boys begged for Andy's story. "I think it's mean," Jamie said. "We didn't find a single clue."

Before there was time for the discussion to grow loud, a teacher noticed them and shooed them to their places. As they scattered to different tables, Chuck angrily whispered that he didn't care what Andy and Sam did, but as for him, he was going to play baseball after school.

Andy and Sam were too happy to care. Sitting at a table with boys from Den One and Den Three, they couldn't talk about their afternoon plans. But they could think about them. Every once in a while, beween bites of sandwich and sips of milk, Sam would say to Andy, "Hurricane," and Andy would answer, "Three forty-seven." It was like having a secret password.

Somehow they lived through the afternoon classes. While Chuck and Bob led the rest of the Den to the playground, Andy and Sam pedaled down Shore Road. This time they passed the McIntyre driveway and rode on to the path nearest Tappan's Landing. Pushing their bikes down the narrow incline, they stacked them carefully, just a few feet from the breakwater. With the marsh grass blowing in the wind, no one standing at the top of the hill or at the Simmses' cottages would ever know that the bikes were there.

"It's like you said," Sam observed. "I didn't promise my mother anything either. But she gave me Hail Columbia for the way my sneakers looked last night. She didn't seem to think we should be fooling around the beach this time of the year."

"Fooling around. Lot they know!" Andy snorted. "Well, we won't get our sneakers wet today for the simple reason that we're going to take them off— right now."

86

The wet sand felt cold as the boys walked over it to the end of the breakwater. Their sneakers, the laces knotted together, were slung around their necks. Climbing to the top of the foremost rock, they looked toward Gull Island. Just below the surface of the water a path of rocks was clearly visible, curving out to the island.

"You sure they go all the way out there?" Sam nervously asked. "I don't see any rocks at the far end."

Andy pulled his Coast Guard map from his pocket and pointed out the outlines of the old carriage road. "Yep, it's all there," he assured Sam. "We just can't see it from here." Consulting his watch, he sing-songed, "The time now is 3:21. In exactly twenty-six minutes it will be low tide."

"Think we should wait?" Sam wondered.

Andy shook his head. "We can see the road now and the tide's going out. We want to get out there as soon as we can, so we can get back before it starts getting high again. Let's roll up our pants."

With their dungarees above their knees, both

boys splashed bravely into the water. It was cold, colder than they had remembered from last summer. But after a squeal or two, they forgot the temperature in the excitement of finding that the road was just where the map said it would be. Once Sam slipped on some seaweed and might have fallen if Andy had not caught his wildly waving arms. Then Andy slipped and Sam caught him, and they landed on Gull Island beach, breathless and laughing.

Eying the underbrush ahead of them, they stopped to put on their sneakers and roll down their dungarees. Before Sam had had time to pick up even one shell, Andy pulled him to his feet.

The roof of the old bath house could be seen through the trees, but there was no path leading to it. Ahead of them a jungle of cat briers covered the ground and threatened to strangle the few blueberry bushes and stunted cedars.

With a silence broken only by an occasional "ouch!" as a cat-brier thorn reached a tender spot or a dead twig scratched a face, the boys plodded through the underbrush. In what seemed like no

88

time at all, they reached the grove of oak trees they had seen from the shore.

In the middle of the grove was a pile of stones. Sam saw it first and made a beeline toward it. Andy, following, lifted the topmost stone and surveyed the heap. The stones made a rough half circle, curving up so that the center was about two feet from the ground.

"Do you suppose this is a marker?" Sam wondered. "Showing where he buried the treasure?"

"It looks to me like those Indian signs pointing to trails," Andy said.

Sitting down, Sam idly sifted the dirt in front of the stones. One small corner of his mind was looking for things—shells, beetles, you never knew what.

"Hey!" Andy suddenly shouted, "look at your hands."

Sam looked down at his hands. They were black, much blacker than the brown soil around him. "They're dirty," he mildly observed.

Andy started to laugh. "That's charcoal and ashes and stuff," he pointed out. "You know what this is? Our Indian sign is only the old fireplace where my father used to cook when he was a boy. What's left of it, anyway."

Wiping his hands on his pants, Sam agreed. Together they walked on to the shack. The door of the old bath house hung at a crazy angle, one hinge rusted away. Swinging the door back, Sam and Andy marched in. For a moment their hands touched as they looked around the room.

A mattress covered with khaki blankets lay on one side of the floor next to a backless chair. At the far end there were rough shelves holding a store of canned goods. Under the lone window stood a rickety table, piled high with opened, rusty cans, with a soiled plate and fork in the center. Everything in the room was covered with cobwebs and dust. Everything looked as if someone had lived there once and had forgotten to come back.

"Achoo," Sam sneezed. "I can't see a thing. It's like night in here."

"Of course you can't," Andy agreed. "Somebody stuffed that window with newspaper."

At the word "newspaper" both boys looked at

each other and then ran for the window. Four eager hands grabbed at the paper, finding it brittle and crumbling to their touch. Carefully they lifted it from the window frame and carried it to the table. The back side of it, the side which had faced outward to the wind and rain, was washed clean, leaving no word visible.

But the inside was clear. Across the top was written in bold, black letters, "THE HUNTSVILLE ENTERPRISE." Beneath it was the date, September 8, 1938.

For a moment Andy and Sam looked at each other, speechless. Then they threw out their arms in a simultaneous effort to pat each other's backs. "Smart brain, smart brain," they howled in chorus.

The newspaper was the extra edition which Mr. Cheyney had published to tell about the bank robbery. But when they looked for the story which they had read in *The Enterprise* office, the article wasn't there. Someone had neatly cut it out with a knife or scissors, leaving everything in the paper but the account of the robbery.

"We've found it. Now I *know* we've found it,"

Andy solemnly announced. "Only somebody who had something to do with the robbery would have cut out that story."

"Now all we have to do is find the money," Sam agreed.

Leaving the paper on the table, the boys toured the cabin. They lifted up the mattress, shook out the blankets, examined each can on the shelf. While Sam tapped on the rough wood walls, Andy balanced himself on the rickety chair and felt along the eaves. In the far corner, almost hidden in the shadows, was another table, with a washbowl and stubby candle on it. When Andy turned the washbowl upside down he found the clipping from *The Enterprise* which described the holdup.

But there were no other clues in the cabin. Nothing in the bed, nothing on the shelf, nothing under the eaves, nothing on the tables.

Sprawling on the mattress, the boys took a final look around. "It's not here," Andy sighed. "I'm sure we're on the right track, but he must have buried it."

"Sure," Sam agreed. "That's where treasure

always is. Buried, I mean. But it's going to be quite a job to dig up this whole old island. Wish we had a clue," and he sneezed again.

"You look as if you'd been working in the bottom of a hole." Andy laughed. "You're a sight—just covered with cobwebs."

"You're not so clean yourself," Sam retorted. "Wait'll your mother sees those pants."

"Holy cow!" Andy looked first at his dungarees, then at his watch. "It's almost five o'clock. We'd better get going if we don't want to swim back." He got up and started slapping the dust off his pants. "Do I look better now?"

Sam shook his head. "You've still got a great big spiderweb on your hair. No"—as Andy slapped his head with his dirty hand—"other side, more to the left."

Andy moved over to the broken mirror above the washbowl. "Gosh, I can't see a thing in here." He blew away the dust from the glass and sneezed noisily. Wiping his nose on his dusty arm, he looked at the mirror again. "Sam!" he howled. "Jeepers, Sam, look here!"

94

Sam leapt from the mattress to Andy's side. "Jeepers," he agreed. Clearly visible on the mirror were some letters, traced there in candle grease.

"What's it say? What's it say?" They elbowed each other in their eagerness.

"19 N 5 W," Andy read off slowly.

"Sounds like a license plate," Sam commented.

Both boys were quiet for a moment. "It's a code," Andy was sure, "like in the Cub book. The numbers stand for letters in the alphabet. Nineteen would be——"

Frantically both boys counted off on their fingers. "1 is A, 2 is B, 3—C, 4—D, 5—E, 6—F," until they reached 19. "S," they shouted together.

"SN," Andy said. "Now for the five."

Again the boys stretched out their fingers. "A—B—C—D—E. Five is E." "SNEW," Andy read off. "Snew. Hey, what's snew?"

"Nothing much. What's new with you?" Sam grinned.

"Oh, ve-r-y funny." Andy's tone was grim. "This is no time for joking. What does S-N-E-W mean?"

Sam shook his head. He was thinking so hard

that the wrinkles were deep on his forehead. "You know, Andy," he finally answered, "maybe it's not a code. Maybe it means feet and directions, like 19 feet north, 5 feet west."

"You've got it!" Andy yelled. "Oh, what a dope I am. Dumb brain," and he clapped his hand to his head. While lifting his arm, he caught another glimpse of his watch. It was now quarter past five.

"We'd better make time," Sam groaned. "We're going to have to swim back."

The slanting rays of the late afternoon sun were glinting on the water as the boys swung back the door of the shack. Without a word, they plunged into the cat briers and fought their way through to the sandy shore. Hastily tying their sneakers around their necks, they stepped into the Sound. The water, which had been ankle-deep when they came out, was now up to their knees.

Sam slipped and fell, landing with only his head above water. Attempting to rescue him, Andy went down too. Thoroughly soaked, they looked at each other and tried to laugh. Through chattering teeth, they groaned, "Our mothers."

96

7 *SALLY LENDS A HAND*

The knob rattled and the hinges seemed to shriek as Andy cautiously opened the side door. For a moment he stood still, sure that his mother must have heard his clatter. But from the kitchen came cooking sounds and the breathless voice of a radio commentator reporting the six-o'clock news. Tiptoeing to safety behind a locked bathroom door, he stripped off his wet clothes and turned on the faucet in the tub.

"Brother, I'm cold," he told himself. "If Mom ever catches me——"

Soaking in the warm bath water, thoughts of buried treasure chased away his worry about his mother. Dreamily he pictured an ancient oaken chest, hooped with brass. There he was with Sam, running his fingers through a mountain of gold pieces. Then the chest shrank to the size of a payroll box and the gold pieces turned into dollars. Five thousand two hundred and ten of them, buried on Gull Island, and he and Sam knew exactly where to find them. Or almost exactly. It would be a cinch to measure off those distances tomorrow and turn up the stolen money.

He was drifting off into another daydream when there was a vigorous banging on the bathroom door. Sitting up hastily, he began to soap himself as the knob turned round and round.

"Hey, Andy," an exasperated voice sounded through the keyhole. "You going to be there all day? What are you doing, anyhow?"

It was Sally, not his mother. Relieved, Andy sank back into the water again. "Taking a bath, stupe. What do you think?"

"Taking a bath?" Obviously Sally didn't believe

98

him. "What's the matter? You sick or something?"

"Oh, ve-r-y funny." Andy groaned. "Can't a person even take a bath without you disturbing him?"

"Listen." Sally had her mouth right at the keyhole now. "I have to fix my hair. There's a Girl Scout meeting after supper. I suppose you're sailing boats or something, but if you don't let me in I'm going to tell Mother. She'll never believe that you're just taking a bath this time of day."

"Sailing boats?" Andy was hurt. "That's kid stuff. I really am taking a bath, like I said."

"Well, you better finish right now," Sally warned. "Mother will be ve-r-y interested to learn that of his own accord Mr. Andrew Hobbs took a bath. Say, maybe you've got a girl."

"A girl?" Andy knew when he was licked. "Be out in a sec. Just give me a chance to dry myself."

Before unlocking the door, Andy pondered the problem of his wet clothes, a salty heap in the middle of the floor. If Sally saw them, he'd be sunk. After a vain attempt to wring them out, he stuffed them in the bottom of the clothes hamper, covering them with his soiled towel. Then he opened the door, bowing mockingly. "Here you are, madam. The bathroom is all yours."

Sally looked him over thoughtfully, noting his damp hair and shiny face. "You really were taking a bath," she decided. "But you're up to something, Andy Hobbs. And I'll find out."

Back in his room, Andy forgot her threat as he started on his homework. The numbers in his arithmetic book danced up and down on the page. Each problem that he tried had the same answer. Multiplication, division, decimals—they all came to 5,210. Slamming the book shut, he picked up his English paper. Usually English was easy.

"Write a sentence using the word 'search.' " Quickly he began, "If we search for the missing money . . ." He stopped himself. "Nope, that's terrible. That'll give me away for sure."

He was chewing on the eraser of his pencil, wondering what to try next, when Sally came in. She had his wet dungarees in her hand. "Told you you were up to something. Wait'll Mom hears about this."

"Tattletale" was on the tip of Andy's tongue,

but he caught himself in time. The situation called for some fast bargaining. "Sally"—he turned on his pleasantest smile—"remember the time when you —ahem—borrowed Mom's gloves and lost them? And I found them? Remember when I saw you downtown when Dad said you had to come home right after school for a punishment? Remember ——" He was beginning to enjoy himself.

"Okay." Sally retreated before his attack. "I won't tell if you'll let me in on it."

"Can't do that. It's a Cub secret."

"Oh, pooh." Teasingly Sally waved the wet pants in the direction of the kitchen. "You'll need my help if you expect to keep these from Mom. She's sure to find them in the morning anyway. You got the whole hamper full of sand."

"Did I?" Andy was worried. "What in heck can I do with them? Sam and I fell into the Sound."

"Didn't take a detective to figure that out," Sally assured him. "It's a wonder Mother can't smell the salt water now. The first thing to do is to get the clothes dry and then brush the sand and stuff off them. I'll hang them in the cellar near the hot-water heater. If——" She paused.

Andy jumped when Sally said "detective." Bursting to tell his story, his last resistance crumbled before her offer of help. "But promise, Girl Scout honor, not to tell?"

Sitting on his bed with his wet pants on her lap, Sally nodded. Her eyes grew wide as he recounted the activities of the last three days. Before he was finished she was gazing at him admiringly. "I've got to hand it to you and Sam. You kids did a wonderful job."

Andy ignored Sally's lofty "you kids." "Don't you think we really have it figured? Can't you just see the faces of those Den One guys when we turn up with the money?"

"We haven't found it yet," Sally reminded him. "I'll bring my compass along tomorrow so we can be sure of the directions."

"What do you mean, 'we'?" Andy bounced down to earth. "You're not in this."

"I'm in it now," Sally corrected him. "Betcha you've never read a compass. You won't even know how to find north and west."

Andy spluttered. "Anybody knows that. When we're on Gull Island, Huntsville is west. North is toward Tod's Point. What do you think the Den will say if I bring a girl along? You're—not—in—this." He was positive.

"Well"—Sally gave in suddenly—"I just remembered that tomorrow I've got to be at the rehearsal for our class play. But you can have my compass. I'll show you how to work it."

"Swell." Having won his point, Andy was properly grateful. "But first help get rid of this—this evidence, will you?"

After tiptoeing down the back stairs to hang Andy's wet clothes in the cellar, Sally returned with her compass. "See, this needle thingamajig always points north——"

"Who doesn't know that?" Andy interrupted. "We learned in Science about the magnetized needle and stuff." He wasn't going to let a girl teach him things, even if she was his sister who was in high school.

Dad's "Hello, everybody" from the front door put an end to the discussion. Hastily pocketing the

compass, Andy rushed to meet him. As he took the steps two by two, he remembered to shout, "Your turn to set the table, Sal." By the time he had relieved Dad of the evening paper to learn that the Dodgers had won, supper was ready.

Conversation at the table was unusually orderly. Most nights Andy and Sally fought for the chance to be heard first, last, and loudest. Mother had long ago appointed herself judge, ruling, "Your turn, Sally. Quiet, Andy," or "Now, Andy, let's hear you. Sally, wait till he's finished." Tonight she and Dad were able to talk without interruption. Sally was wondering whether to skip her rehearsal and surprise the boys on Gull Island, and Andy was back with his treasure-chest daydream. Through a fog he heard his parents mention a new house on the shore.

"Where are they going to build?" Mother wondered. "I thought the Simmses and McIntyres owned all that stretch of land."

"He bought a piece of Simms's property," Dad reported. "Going to start in right away. He hopes to move in before the summer's over."

"Right away?" Andy jumped. "You mean someone's going to start building near Tappan's Landing right away tomorrow?"

"What's the matter with you?" Dad was puzzled by Andy's anguished tone. "I guess not right away tomorrow. He's planning to have some men dig the foundations for the house next week."

"Oh, next week." Andy's relief was apparent to everyone.

"But why do you care?" Dad persisted. Mother looked at him questioningly too.

"I—I don't care." Andy tried to sound offhand. He sent a pleading look in Sally's direction.

"He's just thinking about a treasure hunt he and some of the other children are planning for tomorrow. Bet they've got some clues around the Simmses' cottages," she offered.

Overlooking the "children," Andy gratefully accepted his sister's lead. "Yep, that's it. Didn't want any workmen messing up our clues." To himself he warned, "Keep your mouth shut, Andy Hobbs. You put your foot in it all the time." Except for asking for thirds on dessert—a request his mother promptly denied—he didn't speak another word. As soon as the dishes had been cleared from the table, he excused himself to do his homework.

Trudging up the stairs, he could hear his mother's worried voice. "Something is wrong with that boy tonight. Hope he's not deciding to be sick."

"Not Andy." Sally was positive. "Not the way he ate tonight. Did you see him wolf down those potatoes? Really, Mother, I think you ought to teach him some table manners."

Andy grinned. She was really pretty smart sometimes. Lying in bed after his father called "Lights out," he made plans for tomorrow's expedition. First, get the Den together. Means talking Chuck out of baseball . . . Need shovels and a ruler and Sally's compass . . . Check on low tide . . . So full was he of the things he must remember that he was still tossing about when his parents came upstairs. Punching his pillow and pulling his blanket over his face, he determinedly went to sleep.

The next thing he knew his mother was shaking him by the shoulders to tell him that it was past eight o'clock. Eight o'clock! Andy threw back the blanket and began a mad race into his clothes. He wouldn't have time to talk to the boys before class began unless he could skip eating. But his mother was firm about breakfast. Reluctantly he gulped a glass of juice and tore through a bowl of cereal. Grabbing his jacket from the hook in the front closet, he remembered to call, "G'by. Won't be home till late. It's our—er—treasure hunt today."

Although he pedaled to school at top speed, he knew that he wouldn't be able to catch the Den. "Have to wait till lunch now," he scolded himself. "What a dope!" Entering the classroom just as the bell was ringing, he caught Sam's eye and made a circle with his thumb and forefinger. Sam winked as the class came to attention.

Geography, history, spelling . . . Not even gym this morning, when there would be a chance to whisper to the gang in the corner of the schoolyard. At last the lunch bell buzzed. Inside the cafeteria, Sam and Andy stationed themselves on either side of the door to nudge each Den Two boy as he passed.

108

Catching their excitement, Bob found an empty table in the corner, and Chuck, standing at the dessert counter, steered everyone toward it. By the time Andy and Sam had filled their trays, Den Two was assembled, waiting impatiently for the report.

"Meeting will come to order," Sam announced. His voice was hoarse.

"What's this all about?" Jamie asked.

"Very simple." Andy took a bite of his sandwich while his audience glared. "Very simple. Just that Sam and I know where the stolen money is."

His offhand tone had exactly the effect he'd expected. The table was in an uproar of "Jeepers!" and "Gosh!" and "Where?" and "When?"

"Well, give." Chuck finally made himself heard. "Where is it?"

"We don't exactly have it in our hands yet," Andy explained. "We were patrolling our part of the beach and——" Teasingly, he strung out his story, telling of the horseshoe crab and the search of the Simmses' cottages and his father's report of the 1938 hurricane. By the time he had placed Sam and himself in the shack on Gull Island, the boys were huddled around him. They had even stopped eating.

All except Chuck. He calmly finished his sandwich and started on his ice cream. "Strawberry today," he loudly noted. "My favorite." He was making it clear to everyone that Andy had yet to prove his case.

"Then we found the newspaper in the window with the story of the robbery cut out," Sam took up the tale. "And the clipping was under the washbowl."

Chuck's spoon waved in the air for a moment, then dug down for another load of ice cream. Not until Sam described the writing on the mirror did he give in. With his dessert melting into a pink pool, he began to plan the afternoon's work.

"Everybody meet at my house right after school," he announced. "We can borrow my father's shovels. What time's low tide?"

"Four fifty-one." Andy's answer was prompt. Chuck wasn't going to take over if he could help it. "I have Sally's compass."

"I'll bring Pop's measuring tape," Sam offered.

"But, look," Bob said thoughtfully, "if we all bike to the beach together with shovels and stuff, it will look kind of funny. Besides, Ma said she'd murder me if I got these pants dirty. I have to wear them to my sister's dopey concert on Saturday. I move we go home to get old clothes and meet at the beach. Say four-fifteen."

The rest of the grade was already shuffling out of the cafeteria back to the classrooms. "Second the motion," Pete said.

"Third the motion," Jamie chimed in.

"Okay, four-fifteen at Tappan's Landing," Andy hissed. "Synchronize your watches, men."

8 *NINETEEN FEET NORTH FIVE FEET WEST*

Andy and Sam were the first to arrive at Tappan's Landing. A stiff breeze was blowing up tiny waves along the shore and drying the tops of the big rocks.

"Tide's almost out," Andy noted. "I got the compass. You got the ruler?"

"I *have* it." Sam emphasized the word as he pulled a shiny steel measuring tape from his pocket.

From the path came a "Hey, you guys!" With a shovel precariously balanced in each basket, Chuck

112

and Bob pushed their bikes to the edge of the breakwater. A moment later, Pete hallooed from the top of the hill, then Tim and Jack.

"One, two, three, four, five, six, seven." Bob counted the bicycles stacked in the marsh grass. "Looks like a sale at the Pedal Shop. Where in heck is Jamie?"

With their sneakers slung around their necks, the boys waited impatiently. Sam fished up a piece of seaweed with his big toe, examining it for snails and barnacles, while Chuck and Bob skipped stones across the water. Tim and Jack were picking their way across the first rocks when they heard Jamie's high-pitched, "Hello, fellas."

Dropping his bike, he ran toward them. "Am I late? Ma made me come back and put on a sweater."

"Come on, come on." Chuck waved him to the breakwater. "Get your sneaks off and get moving."

Shouldering a shovel, Andy pushed past Tim and Jack to take the lead. As he sloshed through the cold, ankle-deep water, he pointed out the roadbed to the boys behind him. Chuck, surest of foot, plunged ahead until he was crowding Andy's heels.

"Come on, slowpoke," he teased. "I want to get my hands on that money."

"I want to get my hands on that thousand-dollar reward," Bob called out. "Say, do you suppose the bank'll still give it to us?"

"Oh sure," Pete said. "Let's buy a boat with it."

"Let's buy two boats," Tim suggested.

"Three," Jack called.

"Let's everybody buy a boat. Then we'll have our own Navy," Bob joked.

Jamie looked mournful. "I'm sure Ma'll never let me buy a boat. She says I can't even ride in one till I swim good."

"Well," Sam corrected. He had appointed himself rear guard, keeping one eye on Jamie and the other on a family of ducks swimming beside the breakwater. "Don't worry, Jamie. A thousand dollars won't be enough for eight boats. It's only $125 apiece."

"Only $125?" Tim groaned. "Listen to the man. I've never even seen a hundred dollars. Have you?" and he poked Jack, who was in front of him.

Jack, balancing himself on a seaweedy stretch of rock which the tide had just laid bare, suddenly slipped. He landed on his back in a pool of water. "Whyncha watch what you're doing?" he spluttered.

Before he could stop himself, Tim tripped over Jack's dangling sneakers and joined him in the tidal pool. Bob and Pete, who had been leaping from rock to rock like mountain goats, were next in line, next to slip down in a tangle of legs and arms and seaweed and salt water.

"Four down and four to go." Andy halted to call out the score.

"That's what you think," Chuck shouted. The situation was too much for him. Doubled up with laughter, he tackled Andy. "Touchdown," he shouted triumphantly, as he landed on top of him in the low water.

For a moment Andy was angry. "You got your games mixed. This is the baseball season, not football, you—you—great star, you." Then the sight of the Den sprawled out on the rocks, with only Sam and Jamie left standing, seemed funny. Still sitting in the water, he wadded a handful of seaweed and tossed it at Chuck. "Play ball. Batter up."

Laughing until their sides ached, the boys struggled to their feet again and shook themselves like so many puppies. "You should see yourselves," Jamie giggled. "It's just like a comedy in the movies."

As the sun began to dry out their clothes, they re-formed their line. "Forward, march!" Bob shouted. With sneakers bobbing from their shoulders and shovels held aloft, they made their way across the last stretch of the breakwater.

Jumping down to the beach, Andy made a sweeping bow. "Welcome to Gull Island."

"Betcha I beat to the cabin." Chuck pulled on his sneakers and went crashing through the underbrush.

When the rest of the Den reached the shack, Chuck was already inside, looking at the old copy of

117

The Enterprise. Crowding into the dark and musty room, they fingered the paper, examining the date to see that it sure enough said "September 8, 1938," and studying the blank space where the story of the robbery had been.

"Maybe it's got the man's fingerprints on it," Jamie suggested. "I brought along my magnifying glass in case we needed it for looking at clues."

Bob and Chuck groaned. Without bothering to answer Jamie, they reached for the clipping about the holdup which Sam waved at them, then moved over to study the mirror.

"Here's our big clue." Andy was swelling with pride. "See the writing?"

Each boy took his turn in front of the mirror and each read aloud, "19 N 5 W."

Even Chuck was impressed. "Gosh, this is the real stuff. Come on, fellas. What are we waiting for? Let's go!"

Bob, with a longing look at the cans of food on the dusty shelf, agreed. "Where do we start digging?"

"The problem is where to start measuring from," Sam pointed out. "I think from the door of the cabin, don't you?"

Everyone nodded. Right now the important thing was to get moving. Holding Sally's compass in the palm of his hand, Andy walked to the entrance of the shack. "See"—he pointed to the quivering needle—"this way is north. Now we got to count off nineteen feet."

Sam stretched out the measuring tape toward the north. "That's six feet." Throwing the tape ahead of him, he crawled after it on his hands and knees. "Six feet more. And six more. Makes eighteen. And one foot. Here we are, men. Nineteen feet north." He stood up in a clump of blueberry bushes.

Andy walked along, anxiously following the movements of the compass needle. "Due north." He nodded. "It checks. Now we got to go west." He studied the face of the compass while Sam murmured, "Have to."

Swinging a shovel idly, Chuck was growing impatient. There was something about this business of turning all authority over to Andy and Sam that he didn't like. "Let's have that thing now," he suggested. "Maybe you're reading it wrong."

Andy held tight to the compass, pretending not to see Chuck's outstretched hand. "It's right, all right. Sally showed me how to work it. Start measuring this way, Sam." He turned his back on Chuck to point west.

Chuck liked this less and less. "Gosh, I don't need any Girl Scout to teach me how to read a compass. You're not even holding it straight."

This time Andy didn't answer. He was watching Sam, on his knees again, stretch out the tape for the final measurement. With a sudden grin, Chuck held out his shovel until its blade was directly under Andy's hand. Then he slowly waved it back and forth.

"Say, wait a minute, Sam." Andy sounded puzzled. "There's something funny here. The needle wiggled around and now it looks as if west is over here." He pointed with his left hand. Sam backed into the bushes, preparing to shift his course. "No,

120

wait," Andy said. "Now it moved again. West's in this direction."

"Maybe the compass is broken," Jamie suggested.

Looking doubtful, Andy shook the compass, then lifted it to his ear as if it were a watch. When he held it out again, west was on his right.

Sam crawled out of the bushes to look over Andy's shoulder. As he watched, the needle swung violently around. "Sure does act peculiar," he agreed. Out of the corner of his eye he caught a glimpse of Chuck's slowly moving shovel. "Oh, ve-r-y funny." He pushed the shovel away. "Think you're smart, don't you, Watson?"

Chuck began to laugh, and after a minute Sam joined him.

"I don't get it," Bob wondered. "What's the joke?"

"This dope here——" "The shovel——" Chuck and Sam both started to explain. "There's nothing wrong with the compass," Sam went on. "Chuck was making the needle move by waving the shovel near it."

121

"What's that got to do with it?" Pete asked.

"Well, look." Sam pointed to the compass. "The tip of this needle is magnetized so it will always point north."

"Why?" Jamie interrupted.

"Oh, we had it in Science. About the North Pole, and the earth spinning on its axis and making a magnetic attraction. The magnetized needle always points to the magnetic pole." Sam was patient and professorial.

"I still don't get it." Pete shook his head. "Where does Chuck come in?"

"I did it with my little shovel," Chuck grinned. "Told you I know more about a compass than the rest of you—and your sisters."

"The shovel blade is iron, right?" Sam took over again. "And iron attracts a magnet. Since the compass was a darn sight closer to the shovel than to the North Pole, the needle pointed toward the shovel instead of the Pole."

"Class dismissed," Andy grumbled. "And cut out the fooling, will you, Chuck? We haven't got all day."

"All day? Holy cow, look where that sun is!" Pete pointed through the trees. "Anybody got a watch? I don't want to swim home."

But nobody had a watch and everybody agreed that if they buckled down to business they could locate the spot where they were to dig before taking their chances with the tide. Again Andy pointed west and Sam stretched out his measuring tape.

"One, two, three, four—ouch!" Backing up as he counted, Sam banged his head against the trunk of the tallest oak tree on the island.

"Now we're really stuck." Bob scratched his head. "It's four feet to this tree. Five feet would be right in the middle of it."

"Maybe it's hollow," Jamie said hopefully. "I've heard of people hiding things in hollow trees."

Seven fists thumped the oak. "Nope." Chuck was sure. "Not this baby. This tree is solid wood. We went wrong somewhere."

Before anyone could say "I told you so," Andy walked back to the cabin door. "Have to check the measurements again, men." But when he held out the compass he could barely see the needle. The

123

sun was hidden by the hill along the shore and the island was deep in shadow. He looked questioningly at Sam.

"Better wait till tomorrow," Sam advised. "If I'm late for dinner and soaking wet again——" He left the sentence unfinished.

Disappointed, Andy turned on Chuck. "If you hadn't tried to be a magician, we'd have gotten someplace by now."

Before Chuck could defend himself, Bob picked up the shovels and rule and carried them toward the shack. "Break it up, fellas. Let's stow the equipment and get going."

Following Bob, the Blackhawk Braves tramped to the beach. The trip home was subdued, with each boy absorbed in thoughts of tomorrow. Only Jamie slipped, and Sam, stooping for a shell, managed to catch him before he fell. Back on shore, they laced their sneakers and pushed their bikes up the path. From Shore Road, the sun was a red ball, slipping below the horizon.

"Hey, wait a minute! We haven't decided about tomorrow," Andy reminded them. "The tide won't be low till about quarter to six. That's awful late."

"Awfully," Sam muttered under his breath.

"We could wade," Chuck suggested. "Even if the rocks are under water, we won't get much wetter than we got today. Let's wear shorts so we won't get our pants soaked. Suppose we meet here at four sharp."

"Four o'clock it is," everyone agreed. They mounted their bicycles and raced up the hill toward home.

9 *UP A TREE*

Splashing across the breakwater the following afternoon, the Blackhawk Braves were grimly intent. During Social Studies in school, Johnny Adams had raised his hand to tell about sliding down the firemen's pole and how the alarm system in the firehouse worked. Not to be outdone, Phil Sloane followed with a report of an exciting ride in a police car. When Miss Curran asked about Den Two's visit to *The Enterprise*, there was a long silence. Finally she called on Chuck and he gave a rambling

126

account of the linotype machine and the big press. It didn't sound very interesting, even to Miss Curran, and the smirks on the faces of Den One and Three were unmistakable.

Now the Braves were in full battle regalia. Chuck and Bob had compasses and folding rules borrowed from their fathers' tool tables. Pete and Tim shouldered shovels, and Jack balanced himself on the rocks with a hunting knife strapped to his right hip and a Scout ax to his left. Jamie, still clinging to his magnifying glass, was further fortified with an orange and a banana in each pocket.

Today there was no fooling around as the boys waded across the old carriage road. Following Andy, they marched single file, breaking ranks only when someone slipped on the rocks and grabbed the boy ahead of him for support. In no time at all they were on Gull Island beach, lacing up their sneakers.

"Casualties, one stubbed toe, one scraped shin," Bob sang out. "Clothes and equipment dry. Wearing shorts was a good idea, Chuck."

Wearing shorts seemed less of an inspiration when the boys struck out through the underbrush.

As thorns tore at tender calves and thighs the silent determination which had led them across the rocks in military style dissolved in a chorus of groans. With his ax unsheathed, Jack took the lead, chopping away at the briers.

"Wouldn't you think they'd have put a road in here?" Jamie's voice was an indignant squeak.

By the time the Den reached the grove of oak trees they were ready to call a halt. Squatting around the old fireplace, they pulled out the most persistent prickers and rubbed the sorest spots.

"Hey, General Scherman," Andy nudged Bob. "Next time the army goes on an expedition, better bring bandages."

"I suppose you want a bunch of nurses along, too," Chuck grumbled. He was embarrassed, sure that the others were blaming him for their scratched legs. "What's the matter with you guys? Let's get moving!"

Nodding agreement, Andy walked to the cabin. Before he emerged with a shovel and compass, Chuck and Bob were already at work. The group quickly broke up into three teams of direction-givers and measurement-takers. While Sam backed up on his knees under Andy's orders, Pete followed Chuck's compass reading, and Tim, Bob's. Each boy with a compass and each boy on the ground tried to outshout his rivals. Jack and Jamie, trying to keep from being knocked down, were an impartial cheering section.

"Here!" Sam and Pete shouted at the same moment. With the heels of their sneakers they marked spots on either side of the big oak tree which Sam had bumped into the day before. A few feet away, Bob and Tim were puzzling over the rock to which their measurements had brought them. Each pair stood their ground, sure that they had found the one and only place to dig.

"But, look." Jack tried to reason with them. "You can't all be right."

"Unless he divided up the money and hid it in three different places," Jamie suggested.

United for a moment in explaining to Jamie just how crazy his idea was, the group broke up again into angry argument.

"I don't care about the rest of you," Chuck insisted, "but I'm going to dig on this side of the tree."

Sam was milder but equally firm. "I'm sure we measured right. I think we should dig here."

After striking at his rock with the tip of a shovel, Bob was willing to compromise. "Afraid this is hard as a rock," he grinned. "Look, we'll never get any-where shouting at each other. Why don't we dig on both sides of the tree? That way we'll be sure we're right."

From either side of the oak, Andy and Chuck glared at each other as they broke ground. Scraping away leaves and tossing up stones, they raced to be the first to find the money. But by the time they had dug through the top layer of roots and leaf mold to the softer sand beneath, they were glad to stretch their backs and hand their shovels to Bob and Tim. As each boy took his turn, the holes widened and grew deeper. Once Pete, swinging his shovel hard, heard a ringing sound, as if he'd struck something. At his shout the others crouched down to watch him brush back the dirt with his hands. But it was only a rock, tightly wedged against a sturdy root.

The digging went quickly in the sandy soil. Soon the two holes were big enough for the boys to stand in as they worked. As the piles of tossed-up dirt grew higher, their faces lengthened and their shoulders drooped.

"That guy must have tried to get to China," Chuck grumbled.

Bored with digging, Bob studied the breastworks of dirt on either side of the tree. "Make dandy trenches," he observed. "Why don't we knock off for a while and play war? We could divide into two armies and——"

"No-o-o!" Andy howled. "Positively no. You heard those guys in school today. While they're telling about going to fires and making arrests, do you want to get up at the Pack meeting and say you played soldiers? You can give up if you want to, but I'm going to keep on if——"

"—if it takes all summer," Bob calmly finished for him. "Look, Andy, there must be something wrong. Eight of us have been digging for almost an hour. Our robber was just one man digging alone. He'd have been crazy to go so deep just to bury

131

one small box. We made a mistake somewhere."

"*You* made a mistake—you and your rock," Andy pointed out. "I'm sure Sam and I measured correct."

"Correctly," Sam mildly observed. He had forsaken digging to sit beside the pile of dirt and sift it for white beetle grubs and shiny brown chrysalises. He had half a dozen of each and was wondering how to carry them home without squashing them. "Maybe we did figure this wrong. Because we found those directions written down, we were sure that the robber measured the way we would. But I wonder now if he even had a compass and ruler with him."

The boys were silent, thinking over the meaning of Sam's words. "Are you trying to say," Chuck asked, "that the man would write down those directions without measuring? Just to fool people looking for the money?"

"That's crazy." Bob shook his head. "No one would do that."

"Mean we've just been wasting our time?" Pete moaned. "Oh no-o-o."

"No, look." Sam put down his insects to make his point. "All I mean is we measured those directions accurately—or almost accurately." He glanced at the two holes. "The robber probably just did it roughly, like pacing off nineteen feet and five feet."

"Sure." Andy was catching on. "He just walked north and west, not due north or due west, like the compass shows. He'd have a gun and stuff for holding up the bank, but he wouldn't think about getting a compass and ruler like we did."

Chuck was doubtful. "Then all we have to do is take nineteen steps one way and five the other? Sounds too easy to me."

"It's kind of tricky," Sam pointed out, "because our steps wouldn't be as big as the robber's."

"Hey, wait. We know how tall he was. It's in the paper." Bob was on Sam's side now. "We should be able to figure something from that."

There was a mad dash for the cabin. Chuck read aloud from the clipping describing the holdup. "According to Mr. Odell, the robber was about five foot ten."

133

"But the body was shorter," Bob interrupted.

Everyone stared at Bob, mystified. "That doesn't make any sense," Jamie squeaked.

"Oh, you know what I mean," Bob explained. "The man on the beach at Tod's Point. The drowned one. I remember he was five foot eight."

"Smart brain." Sam nodded. "That would be the right measurement, of course."

"If we're right about any of this," Chuck pointed out.

"You wanna quit?" Andy thrust his chin in Chuck's direction. The freckles on his nose were beginning to pop out, and his hair seemed a brighter red.

"Well no, but——"

"But what?"

"Knock it off, you two." Bob's voice was firm. "What do you always want to be fighting about?"

Andy's chin dropped back to normal position. "Wasn't fighting. But just as we're getting somewhere, Chuck's always got a complaint."

"Wasn't com——"Chuck started until Sam put his hand over his mouth. "We have a job for you,

Chuck," he explained diplomatically. "You're the biggest so you'll have to do the pacing. How tall are you?"

"Five feet two." Chuck stretched himself to his full height. "I'm almost as tall as my mother."

Sam was scratching his head. "That still leaves you six inches shorter than the robber. Let's see you walk."

Obediently Chuck started off through the woods.

"Whoa!" Sam called him back. "Now try taking big steps. Walk back and forth here so we can all watch you. No"—as Chuck began to leap across the ground—"the man wasn't a giant. He was about as big as your father."

Chuck paced in front of the cabin, varying the size of his footsteps while the rest of the boys shook their heads. "Well, make up your minds," he muttered.

"I've got an idea," said Andy. "When I go walking with my father I take extra big steps to keep up with him. Could you pretend you were walking with your father, Chuck, and keep step with him, sort of?"

135

Chuck thought a moment, then nodded. Back and forth he paraded until his anxious critics were sure that he had achieved the proper manly stride.

"Okay." Sam turned him facing north. "Now walk like that and we'll count nineteen steps."

"I feel like It in Blind Man's Buff," Chuck complained. "Let's get this over with." He walked carefully, intent on keeping the proper distance between his two feet. A chorus of voices counted off, "One, two, three, four." When they shouted "Nineteen," he stood stock-still, teetering on the balls of his feet.

"Now this way." Sam turned him toward the water. Again the boys counted. At "Five," Chuck looked up to find himself under the big oak tree, only a few feet from the holes they had been working on. He stood motionless until Bob produced a shovel and pointed it at his feet. Andy dug too, while the rest of the Den watched in silence. This time for sure, each one thought.

The hole grew deep, but there was no sign of a box. Perspiring and a little discouraged, Andy and Bob stopped to catch their breath. Pete and Chuck took over, then Tim and Jack. The waiting Braves squatted listlessly around the excavation, examining their blisters and beginning to think of retreat. Jamie fished the oranges and bananas from his pocket and distributed them as evenly as he could. But the taste of food only made them more dejected.

"Boy, what I wouldn't give for a cold glass of soda right now," Tim mourned.

"Boy, what I wouldn't give for a whole bottle," Jack said wistfully.

"Betcha I could drink a gallon," Chuck topped them.

Feeling that his dream was about to collapse, Andy picked up a shovel again and vigorously attacked the hole. He was angry now—angry at the robber, angry at himself, angry at the other boys, who seemed ready to desert him. Even Sam had moved around to the far side of the tree and was picking at the furrowed bark with his fingernails, in search of carpenter ants. "Bugs!" Andy muttered to himself.

Noting his bristling hair and the way the freckles

137

showed on his sweaty face, Chuck sighed. "I know what you're going to say, Andy, but this is hopeless. We're not getting anywhere."

Andy glared. He threw a shovelful of dirt on the pile. "You want to give up again?"

Bob came to Chuck's defense. "No one wants to give up," he soothingly explained, "but we don't seem to turn anything up."

"Up, up, that's all you can say!" The more doubtful Andy felt, the angrier he became. "We're supposed to be digging down, not up. All you guys sitting around——" He dug another shovelful of dirt.

"Up, up." Absent-mindedly listening to the argument, Sam leaned his head back to look at the topmost branches of the oak tree. There was a nest up there, a great mound of dried leaves and twigs, tucked securely in a crotch between the main trunk and a heavy limb. Sam flopped to the ground and thought a moment.

"Hey, fellas," he called. "Maybe we've been going in the wrong direction. Look up here."

Without much hope, the boys craned their necks

to follow Sam's pointing finger. Andy continued with his digging, determined to ignore the lot of them.

"All I see is an old bird's nest," Bob observed. "So what?"

Sam sighed. "It's not a bird's nest. It's a squirrel's. Much bigger than a bird's, except maybe a crow's. In the winter the squirrels live in hollow trees, but in summer they build these nests out of leaves and——"

He was ready to continue with a short talk on the home life of the gray squirrel when Chuck cut him off. "Birds, squirrels—sometimes I think you're nuts, Sam. What's this got to do with finding buried treasure?"

"Listen to the birdie. Tweet, tweet, tweet!" Pete mocked. Everyone felt cross now, and ready to quarrel.

Sam's voice was hoarse, but his reply was still patient. "We keep thinking about this money as if it were pirate gold. But we're looking for real United States dollar bills, hidden by a bank robber. There's no law that would make him *bury* them."

Tossing down his shovel, Andy leapt over a mound of dirt to join the group under the tree. "Go on, Sam, explain," he urged.

"Look," Sam continued. "Each time we measure we end up at this tree. Well, what do you think about first about trees?"

"Climbing them," Jamie answered promptly.

"Right." Sam nodded. "Suppose the robber climbed the tree and hid the money in the squirrel's nest?"

"I can't see a thing up there," Bob objected. "It just looks like a pile of leaves."

"It's hollow inside," Sam explained. "The leaves on top are like a roof to keep the rain out."

"I move we climb the tree and look in the nest," Andy suggested. "All in favor say 'Aye.' "

There was a faint chorus of "Ayes." Chuck just sat and shook his head.

"Jamie, you're the lightest," Pete said. "We'll boost you and you climb up and look in the nest."

Andy clasped his hands and held them low for Jamie to step on while Pete and Sam shoved him upward until he could reach the first branch. He climbed slowly, hand over hand, pulling himself along the massive trunk. The boys at the foot of the tree watched in silence. They could hear the scraping of his sneakers on the rough bark and the squawking of the gulls offshore. At last he was high enough. A few dry leaves floated down as he poked his hand into the squirrel's nest. Seven Blackhawk Braves held their breath.

"It's here," Jamie called. "It's here."

"Shush." Andy tried to silence the shrieks. "What's there, Jamie? What do you see?"

"A box about so big." Jamie wedged himself against the trunk so he could show them with his hands.

"Pick it up!" "Hold it up!" "Let's see it!" Everyone shouted at once.

Cautiously, Jamie braced his feet and reached into the nest. When his hand reappeared it was waving a dusty, green metal box with silver handles. At the sight of it there was a blast of noise from the base of the tree.

"Smart brain!" Andy gave Sam a hearty clap on the shoulder.

141

"Smart brain, smart brain." Sam grinned back at him.

As the hubbub subsided, Chuck began to assert himself. "Throw the box down, Jamie. I'll catch it."

"I will not." Jamie was indignant. "I climbed up after it and I'm going to bring it down."

"Use your belt," Andy shouted. "Tie the box to you with your belt."

With every eye on him, Jamie unbuckled his belt and passed it through the handles of the box. Then he looped the belt around his neck so that the box bobbed between his shoulder blades. Slowly he made his way down, hugging the trunk with his body and feeling along the branches with his hands and feet. When he reached the lowest branch he turned around and faced the group.

"Jump," Chuck suggested. "Bob and I will make a seat for you."

Jamie looked doubtful. He watched Chuck and Bob cross wrists and clasp hands.

"Jump," Chuck repeated. "Don't worry. We won't let you fall."

"Jump into the human net, the only living human net! See the daredevil, death-defying leap!" Bob tried to encourage him by imitating the ringmaster in the circus.

Closing his eyes, Jamie suddenly jumped. Chuck and Bob, who hadn't expected him so soon, failed to brace themselves. Their shoulders caved in and down they went, with Jamie on top of them. Before they could unscramble their legs, Andy had pounced on the box.

"Lemme have it!" "Lemme see it!" everyone demanded.

"I'm going to open it." Andy shielded the box from the row of outstretched hands.

"It's not fair," Jamie protested. "I found it. I should be the one to open it."

"Where's the key?" Sam pointed out. "We can't open it without a key."

Andy poked at the lock with his fingernail. Then eight hands reached into eight pockets for eight knives. As Andy put down the box to open his knife, Chuck picked it up. He worked the point of his blade into the keyhole.

"Too big." He shook his head. "Need something smaller."

This time pockets were turned inside out and their contents piled on the ground. Paper clips, rubber bands, fish hooks, bits of string, orange peelings, nails.

"Try a nail," Sam suggested. "That ought to fit."

Fumbling through the pile, Chuck selected the longest, thinnest nail. It slid easily into the keyhole, but it didn't turn the lock. The boys squatted back on their heels.

"So near and yet so far," Bob mourned.

"Why not take it to the bank and ask them to open it?" Jamie suggested.

Pete gave him a disgusted look, and listed the reasons why this was not a good idea. He ended up with a shout, "WE WANT TO BE THE FIRST TO SEE THE MONEY."

"Guess the only thing to do is break the lock," Sam said. "If we hold the nail in the keyhole and hammer it in with something——"

Before Sam finished the sentence, Andy, armed with a flat stone, was whacking away at the nail. As

145

it slid in up to its head, the boys could hear the lock give way. Prying the nail out, Andy lifted the silver handles. There was a stack of green-and-white bills in the open box.

"Oh boy!" "We've got it!" Eager fingers reached out for the money. Chuck pushed everyone back.

"Cut it out," he ordered. "We don't want to lose any of the treasure. General Scherman, will you count it?"

Sam and Andy exchanged annoyed glances as they watched Bob lift out the money. From the top of the pile he took a hundred-dollar bill and held it up for them all to see. Then another and another and another. "Five hundred, six hundred, seven hundred." Slowly he counted until he had reached one thousand. Then came the fifty-dollar bills. A second thousand, a third. Then the twenties. "Twenty, forty, sixty, eighty, one hundred. Three thousand and one hundred dollars," Bob sing-songed. The stack of bills in the box grew smaller. "Four thousand dollars," he announced, then "five thousand dollars."

"Five thousand dollars." The boys sighed. The

rest of the money was in single dollars, and Bob began to tire of his job. Twice he forgot what number he had reached and had to start back at the beginning. As he neared the bottom of the pile, his audience chanted with him, "$5,201, $5,202, $5,203, $5,204, $5,205, $5,206, $5,207, $5,208." And that was all.

"Hey, it's two dollars short," Pete said.

"Probably the robber spent the money," Jamie squeaked.

"Couldn't have." Andy shook his head. "Remember, they knew the numbers of the bills and none of them were ever turned in. Probably General Scherman counted wrong. Here, Sam"—he lifted the pile of bills from Bob's lap—"you check it now."

While Sam counted, the other boys stretched out on the ground beside him. "Wonder when we'll get the reward." Tim's voice was dreamy.

"Think we should take the money to the bank in the morning or call Mr. Oakley when we get home tonight?" Jack asked.

"I think we should give the money to Mr. Chey-

147

ney," Jamie said. "We'd never have found it if we hadn't gone to *The Enterprise*."

"Tomorrow's Saturday and the bank is closed," Chuck pointed out. "I suppose we could call Mr. Oakley when we get home, but——"

"*When* we get home?" Andy interrupted. "More like *if*. Look how dark it is."

With a start, the boys sat up and looked around. The oak grove was always in shadow, but they could see that the sun had left the water. Far away on the horizon, the sky was faintly pink. Directly above them it was a deepening blue, rapidly shading to black. One star was clearly visible.

"Holy cow, no wonder I'm so hungry!" Bob exclaimed. "It's way past suppertime!"

Sam snapped down the lid of the money box. "All here," he announced. "I make it exactly $5,210. Let's go."

"Look around you, Sammy boy," Andy advised. "Just what time would you say it is?"

Sam looked up at the darkening sky, then through the trees at the water and distant shore. He gulped. "The tide! It'll be halfway in."

The tide! The boys plunged into the underbrush, forgetting thorns in a mad rush for the shore. Sam, stopping to scoop up the box of money, was the last to leave the oak grove. By the time he reached the beach, he found a silent group, straining to find signs of the old carriage road. The water had risen, and in the darkness which now surrounded them, it was impossible to see even the nearest rocks of the breakwater. The Huntsville beach was far away and the water looked black and cold.

"We could swim," Chuck halfheartedly suggested.

"I can't swim." Jamie's voice broke a little. "All I can do is dead man's float."

10 MAROONED

The Blackhawk Braves straggled back toward the cabin, feeling their way through the cat briers with the light of a quarter-moon to guide them.

"Brother, we're in for it," Andy groaned.

"You can say that again." Bob shook his head. "I can just imagine what my mother will say. *And* my father."

"I hate to imagine what my mother will say," Pete wailed.

"It's going to be fierce," Tim agreed.

150

"We can get home before breakfast." Sam tried to comfort them. "Tide'll be low just as it begins to get light."

"Before breakfast!" Jack was glum. "You ought to hear my mother if I don't get home before dinner."

"Look, fellas, we're not so badly off," Andy said. "Our families will give us what for, but they're going to feel pretty proud of us when we show up with the stolen money."

"Sure, and don't forget the reward," Pete added.

"You know what I think?" Jamie began to cheer up. "I think we're real heroes. Like in a book."

"Personally, I'm a hungry hero," Chuck said. "What do they do in books when they're lost in the woods without any supper?"

"We're not lost in the woods," Sam pointed out.

"Well, marooned on a desert island, then. What's the diff?" Chuck asked.

Sam took the question seriously. "On a desert island there are always things to eat—berries and nuts and wild game that they shoot with the bows and arrows they make. But no berries and nuts are ripe yet. I read someplace that the Indians used to eat jack-in-the-pulpit root, but you have to boil it a long time or it's very bitter."

"Well, we've got a long time. All night. My stomach is howling for food," Bob said.

"Let's see." Sam was still pondering the problem. "When Tom Sawyer lived on an island, he brought along a ham and they caught some fish. The Swiss Family Robinson and Robinson Crusoe tamed goats and ate breadfruit and stuff like that. But at first they just swam out to their wrecked ships and got provisions from there."

"That's it!" Andy shouted. "Why didn't I think of it before? Dumb brain!" and he clapped his hand to his head.

"What's it?" Chuck sounded exasperated. "I'm starving to death."

Andy sprinted toward the cabin. "The shipwreck," he called over his shoulder. "We don't have a ship but we have a shack. Remember the cans of food, you dopes?"

The boys tumbled after him into the dark cabin,

tripping over the ramshackle chair and stubbing toes on the mattress in the corner. The moon shone faintly through the cracks in the roof. As their eyes became accustomed to the darkness, Andy and Chuck found the shelf of canned goods.

"Where there's a can there must be a can opener," Chuck muttered.

"I remember seeing one on the table," Sam said.

Bob felt carefully around. "Yep, here it is. And here's his pot. Bet it's awful dirty, though."

"Let's cook outside in my dad's old fireplace," Andy suggested. "We'll get wood for a fire while you take the pot down to the water and wash it out."

"Okay." After turning the can opener over to Chuck, Bob struck out for the beach with the pot in his hand. The rest of the boys walked toward the oak grove, each carrying a can. Before Sam left, he lifted the corner of the mattress and shoved the box of money underneath it.

It took only a few minutes to collect a pile of twigs and dead branches. "Got enough light wood now, fellas," Chuck announced. "What we need are a couple of heavy logs so we can have a really hot fire. Be good if we could keep it going all night."

"Getting kind of cool already." Tim flapped his bare arms around his chest.

"Cool and mosquitoey." Jack gave his leg a resounding slap.

There were footsteps in the underbrush. "Halt! Who goes there?" Andy called out. "Give the password or be prepared to die."

"Oh, ve-r-y funny," Bob breathlessly replied. "One of you guys give me a hand. I found a whole pile of boards washed up on the beach. I've got a whopper here but it keeps getting stuck in the briers."

Andy helped Bob carry the board to the fireplace. "Must be from a wrecked ship. Just like Robinson Crusoe, Sam."

"Look," Bob suggested, "suppose you get the fire going while Pete and I go back to the beach for more wood. With a decent blaze we'd be able to find our way through this jungle."

Chuck let out a shout. "*Get the fire going?* WHO'S GOT MATCHES?"

154

Jamie broke the horrified silence. "We could rub two sticks together like the Indians."

"Yeah, and be here all night," Pete said gloomily. "Did you ever try rubbing two sticks together in the dark?"

"Well, we're going to be here all night anyway," Sam pointed out. "I read in the Boy Scout Handbook about making a fire set. You cut a hole in a board and put a stick in the hole, and then you make a bow from a piece of leather and——"

"Oh no," Bob groaned. "Save that for shop class. I move we open the cans and eat the stuff cold. My stomach is positively standing on end."

Andy had a sudden thought. Frantically he searched his pockets. Then, with a broad grin, he held up a small metal box. "Matches, and they're dry, too. They're the kind for camping trips."

"Where'd you get them?" Sam asked. "Never saw you with those before."

Andy hesitated. "They're from Sally's Girl Scout stuff. I—ahem—borrowed them from her this morning."

"Well, let's have them." Chuck held out his hand. "Never thought I'd be thankful for Girl Scouts. I'll start the kindling while Pete and Bob go after those boards."

On the second match, a twig caught fire. Soon the kindling was ablaze. Chuck and Andy piled on branches until the fire lit up the whole grove. Then they placed Bob's board on top.

"It's a little wet," Andy said, "but it'll burn."

"It has to," Chuck replied.

As the flames cut through the darkness, the rest of the boys took turns with the can opener.

"What have you got?" Tim held his can toward the light. "Mine's beans."

"Mine's beans," Jack called.

"Beans." "Beans." There was an echo around the half circle of stones.

"Guess this is what they call being full of beans," Tim joked.

"Full of beans! Wish we were. I am about to perish of starvation." Dramatically, Jack threw himself to the ground, his hand clutching his stomach.

156

"Well, what are we waiting for? Let's dump them in the pot." Andy held out the pot while Sam emptied the contents of the cans into it. "Still got four left," he announced when the pot was full.

"Stand them inside the fireplace and the beans will warm up in the cans," Sam suggested.

"Good idea," Chuck agreed, "but be careful of them. They'll get awful hot."

"Awfully," Sam corrected, but Chuck ignored him.

When Pete and Bob returned from the beach with a load of boards, the boys were sitting cross-legged around the fire, passing the pot from hand to hand so that each could take his turn at shaking it over the flames. Bob leaned over and stuck his finger in. Licking it off, he pronounced the beans ready to eat. "Done to perfection." He smacked his lips.

"We haven't any plates or spoons," Jamie pointed out.

"I suppose you want a tablecloth and napkins, too," Chuck answered. "What do you suppose you have fingers for?"

The boys lined up and Chuck filled their empty cans with steaming-hot beans. Then Bob and Sam and Andy shared the pot with him. All conversation ceased. Each Brave raced to finish his portion. When cans and pot were empty and sticky fingers had been licked clean, they turned to the extra cans inside the fireplace.

"Ouch! They're hot. How are we going to pick them up?" Bob called.

"Anybody got a handkerchief?" Andy sounded doubtful.

Jamie fished a folded square from his pocket. "My mother made me take it," he apologized.

Nodding sympathetically, Andy held the hot cans with Jamie's handkerchief and divided the remaining beans. "Never tasted anything so good in my life," he mumbled as he stuffed three fingerfuls into his mouth.

Soon there wasn't a bean to be found on Gull Island. The fire was bright and comfortable, and eight sleepy boys stretched out around it, pillowing their heads on crossed arms. Every once in a while someone sat up to toss another branch on the glowing coals. Then orange flames spurted out and a fountain of sparks rose to the top of the oak trees.

"Boy, this is the life," Bob sighed. "I wish we could stay here all summer. Tenting tonight on the old camp ground. Hey, anybody want to sing?"

No one did. They were content to lie back and look up at the trees and sky. Fighting to keep awake, Jamie lifted his head from his hands. "Let's wish on a star. What do you wish, Pete?"

"Wish on a star!" Chuck imitated Jamie's squeaky voice. "Why don't you grow up?"

Ignoring Chuck, Pete dreamily began, "I wish ——" Abruptly he sat up and slapped his legs with both hands. "I wish I could kill every last mosquito in the world."

Pete's mosquito buzzed from leg to leg and the Braves rose to do battle. Arms tangled and hands hit against bare thighs. "Got it!" Sam finally shouted.

The boys stretched out again, but the peaceful mood was gone.

"I'm so thirsty I could drink the Sound," Bob complained.

"The Sound's salty," Sam reminded him.

"Well, then I wish I had a gallon of orange pop and when that's gone I wish I had a gallon of ice-cold water."

"Look's like you're going to get your wish," Chuck said. "The second part anyway. It's starting to rain."

A dark cloud had covered the moon and the stars. Rain began to fall, at first hesitantly, then in big determined drops. The boys opened their mouths to catch the welcome water, then watched in dismay as the fire hissed and sizzled and died out. With chattering teeth, they ran for the cabin.

The shack was dark, darker than it had been outdoors, and through the cracks in the roof and the broken window a steady stream of rain pelted in. It was impossible to see anything, and they stumbled around in the tiny room, hunting for a place to sit. Bob plunged headlong into the table, and rusty cans tumbled to the floor with a clatter which made everyone jump. After Andy pulled the mattress away from the wall to a spot near the door which was almost dry, the boys felt their way toward it. Huddling together, they stretched out the two mildewed blankets until each had a share of the covering. With wet hands they rubbed rain water from their wet heads.

"Hey, we could get good money for this place," Chuck tried to joke. "For rent, cabin with running water and built-in shower."

Jamie sneezed. No one spoke for a long time. The Blackhawk Braves were suddenly cold and tired and miserable.

"How long do you suppose this rain will last?" Bob broke the silence.

Pete sighed. "Probably all night."

"When it comes down this hard it usually lets up quickly," Sam assured them.

"Then we can build the fire again." Andy tried to sound cheerful.

"If we can find any dry wood, which I doubt," Chuck pointed out with painful practicality.

Again there was silence, broken by an occasional sneeze. From the corner of the mattress where Jamie sat, suspicious sniffles could be heard.

"What time do you suppose it is?" a doleful voice inquired.

"Oh, at least midnight," Andy answered. "We've only got about five more hours."

"Midnight! *Only* five more hours!" Jamie's sniffles were now definitely sobs. "I want to go home. I want my mother."

In their hearts, the other boys felt like Jamie. Each was ready to trade his hero's role for a familiar warm bed any time someone offered to make the exchange. But they would rather face boiling in oil than admit it. Sam put his arm around Jamie's quivering shoulders, and Bob gave his knee a sympathetic pat.

"Everything's going to be all right," they tried to reassure him. "Just think about tomorrow and the money and the reward."

"Oh boy, I just can't wait for those guys in Den One and Den Three to hear about this." Chuck tried hard to sound as if he meant it.

"Maybe we'll be rescued yet," Sam hoped. "Lots of times people marooned on desert islands get rescued."

162

"Who'll rescue us?" Jamie stopped crying to ask. "No one knows where we are."

"Hey, listen. I think I hear something." Andy was suddenly alert.

Sure that he was just trying to cheer up Jamie, the others ignored him. The rain had slackened. Now it was making only faint pit-pat sounds on the roof.

"Listen!" Sam's voice was hoarse.

The boys strained to follow his direction. From the far end of the island they thought they could hear a faint "Halloo, halloo." Then there were sounds of tramping in the underbrush. Somebody— or something—was definitely moving toward them.

Throwing the blankets from their shoulders, they crowded together at the door. Beyond the trees, a sharp beam of light, then another, pierced the darkness. Two flashlights were waving along the path.

"Who goes there?" Chuck cupped his hands around his mouth.

"Hello!" came an answering call. "Where are you? Are you all right?"

163

"Dad! Dad!" Andy shouted. "We're at the cabin, your old cabin."

Even Jamie was convinced that a rescue party was on its way. Forgetting the rain, which had slowed down to a drizzle, they ran toward the flashlights. At the fireplace, the two groups met. Andy and Chuck hurled themselves into their fathers' arms. Holding tight to Andy, Mr. Hobbs turned his light on the bedraggled boys.

"Are you all here, all all right?" he anxiously asked.

"Just fine, Dad," Andy assured him. "If it hadn't been for the rain we'd be in great shape." Suddenly he remembered the purpose of their expedition. "We found the treasure. We found the missing money."

"We're heroes," Jamie piped.

As soon as they knew that the boys were safe, Mr. Hobbs and Mr. Watson were angry. "Heroes!" Chuck's father exploded. "We'll see about that tomorrow. Right now you're going home to bed. Your mothers and fathers are all frantic."

Taking Andy by the hand, Mr. Hobbs led the

way to the shore. "We'll have *plenty* to see about tomorrow." He emphasized the word. "We've even got the police out hunting for you. Sure you were drowned or run over or something."

Tomorrow promised to be quite a day. Subdued, the boys tramped through the briers. The McIntyres' boat was pulled up on the beach. Mr. Watson held the bow and flashed his light while they clambered in. "There are blankets under the thwarts. Put them around you," he ordered.

"How'd you find us, Dad?" Andy asked as his father fiddled with the motor.

"Your sister Sally finally told us some wild story about buried treasure on Gull Island. She wouldn't say a word until after it started to rain. Said she'd promised, Girl Scout honor, not to tell." Mr. Hobbs's voice was grim.

He yanked on the starter cord. The motor went putt-putt, then stopped, then went putt-putt again.

Suddenly Sam let out an agonized scream. "The money! It's still in the cabin. Mr. Hobbs, Mr. Watson," he pleaded, "you've got to let us go back for it."

"We've had enough of your games for one day."
Chuck's father shook his head. "You're not going
any place but bed."

Slowly the boat turned and headed for the shore.
Eight Blackhawk Braves groaned in chorus.

11 *EXTRA! EXTRA!*

The sun was high in the sky when Andy woke. Sitting up in bed, he tried breathing through his nose. The result was very much like a snort. He sneezed. He cleared his throat with a gruff "Hem, hem." He sneezed again.

Pushing open his door, Sally rushed in. "Did you find it? I've been dying for you to wake up. Dad's mad at me too and he wouldn't say a thing."

Between sneezes, Andy nodded.

168

"Wonderful." Sally flopped on his bed. "Tell me all about it. You've got an awful cold," she added sympathetically.

Wiping his streaming eyes and nose, Andy described yesterday's expedition. Sally listened without interrupting, even when he told about her matchbox. When he finished, she had only one question. "Where's the money?"

Andy combined a sneeze and a moan. "It's still on the island. We forgot it."

"You forgot five thousand dollars?" Sally couldn't believe it. "You forget your jacket or your homework or to go to the dentist, but nobody— nobody could forget five thousand two hundred and ten dollars."

Andy looked a little embarrassed. "We didn't exactly forget it," he defended himself. "Sam hid it in the cabin when it got dark. When Dad came we ran out to meet him and then he wouldn't let us go back for it."

The thought of his father had a sobering effect on Andy. "How are things this morning?" He pointed in the direction of the living room.

"Bad." Sally shook her head. "You know how mothers and fathers are. They just won't listen. I tried to tell them about the bank money, but they kept thinking you were playing a treasure-hunt game. By the way, I'm sorry about breaking my word, but they were so worried. When it rained I guess I got worried, too."

Andy brushed off her apology with a wave of his hand. Sally's unexpected sympathy and admiration made him feel important. Being a hero to his big sister was a new experience and a pleasant one. "Guess I better get up and get the bawling out over with."

Sneezing heartily, he made his way to the bathroom. As he squeezed a generous dab of toothpaste onto his brush, the telephone rang downstairs. Listening, Andy realized that his mother was talking about him.

"—still upstairs asleep." . . .

"Why, I don't know. I don't know what you're talking about." . . .

"Oh no. Just something they'd buried for their Cub Scout treasure hunt." . . .

"I didn't talk to him last night. He was so wet and tired that I put him right to bed." . . .

"I'm sure you're wrong. But wait. I'll put my husband on the phone. He was on the island with them."

Still grasping his toothbrush, Andy tiptoed to the head of the stairs. Who could be on the other end of the telephone? His mother answered the question for him.

"Tom," she called in a puzzled voice. "Mr. Cheyney of *The Enterprise* is on the phone. He's asking about the treasure the boys found. Something about money stolen from the bank."

Dad's deep voice took up the conversation. With increasing irritation he kept repeating, "No, no real money. Just kid stuff." . . .

"You know how we used to hunt for the pieces of eight that Captain Kidd buried." . . .

"No, no—fool's gold is more like it."

Andy, halfway down the stairs, sneezed indignantly. Fool's gold indeed!

His father looked up from the phone. "Andrew, come right here and talk to Mr. Cheyney," he commanded. "Explain to him about your Cub treasure hunt."

Barefooted and still in his pajamas, Andy hopped down the steps. With a glance at his red eyes and damp nose, his mother tried to send him back for his slippers.

"No," his father insisted. "Let's get this settled first, even if he has to stay in bed for a week. Every fool and his brother has been calling up about this nonsense all morning." He handed the telephone to Andy.

"Hello, Mr. Cheyney." Andy's tone was jubilant. "We found the money, every last penny of it. Five thousand two hundred and ten, just like *The Enterprise* said." His chest puffed out, then caved in as a sneeze overtook him.

"Nope, not buried. Up a tree. In a squirrel's nest."

"Well"—his manner became offhand—"guess you could say it was good detective work on Sam's and my part. But all the fellows helped. Be sure to put in that all the fellows helped."

In response to a question from the other end of

the wire, Andy turned to his parents. They were staring at him, open-mouthed. "All right if Mr. Cheyney comes right over? He wants to interview me for the paper. Probably take my picture, too."

His parents nodded weakly, then lowered themselves into nearby chairs. Sally, who had been listening on the stairs, walked down to join them.

By the time Andy hung up the receiver he seemed to have grown inches taller, even in his bare feet. He turned to face his parents. "Sorry you were worried about us last night. We didn't mean to stay, but——"

"WHAT"—his father's voice shook the room— "IS THIS ALL ABOUT? Did you really find five thousand dollars?"

Andy grinned and nodded. A little uncertainly, he began the story of the Know-Your-Neighborhood project. By the time he reached Gull Island, some fifty sneezes later, he was swinging his legs from his father's big chair and gesturing with his father's best linen handkerchief. Sally had been sent for his bathrobe and slippers, and his mother

174

was on her way from the kitchen with a breakfast tray. Andy was enjoying himself.

His parents waited patiently while he drank his orange juice and went to work on an egg. Then, nibbling a doughnut, he continued with his tale. As he was describing Jamie's descent from the tree with the box, the doorbell rang.

"Good morning," Mr. Cheyney's pleasant voice boomed. "Where's that detective fellow of yours?"

Mr. Cheyney joined Andy's audience. At the end of the story, he rose to shake his hand. "Congratulations, son. A fine piece of work."

"Smart brain." Sally smiled at him.

His mother and father were still not sure how they felt. "It was a good job," Mr. Hobbs agreed. "You and Sam and the rest showed great ingenuity and persistence. But you were also downright thoughtless and disobedient."

"Might have gotten pneumonia," Mrs. Hobbs added as Andy sneezed again.

"I know how you feel," Mr. Cheyney interceded. "I have a boy myself, although he's a grown man now, with a family of his own. But Andy and

175

the others didn't mean anything wrong. They just had bad luck with the tides. You know, if he'd told you about it ahead of time you never would have believed they'd find the money. I was certainly sure they wouldn't."

Andy nodded vigorously. "Never do it again," he promised.

"I'll have to think about it." Mr. Hobbs sounded almost convinced. "But speaking of the money, where is it, Andy? Mr. Cheyney ought to check the numbers on the bills."

Andy's face fell. "It's still on Gull Island. You wouldn't let Sam get it." He explained about hiding it in the cabin.

Mr. Hobbs burst into laughter. "You spend a week finding this money, doing all sorts of clever things and working your heads off. Then, at the last minute, you just forget it." Noticing Andy's hurt face, he stopped. "Never mind, Son. We'll get it now. Run up and put your clothes on while I see if I can borrow McIntyre's boat again."

While Mrs. Hobbs protested about the effect of the Sound air on Andy's cold, he went upstairs to

176

dress. "How'd I do?" he whispered to Sally when they were out of earshot of the grownups.

"Fine," she assured him. "When Dad says he has to think about something, it always comes out all right."

"What's ingenuity?" Andy asked. " 'Ingenuity and persistence,' Dad said."

Sally thought a moment. "It means like—like 'smart brain.' "

Andy smiled to himself as he pulled his shirt over his head. Half an hour later he had assembled the Blackhawk Braves for the trip to Gull Island. Only Jamie was missing. Over the telephone his mother had explained that she was keeping him in bed until his cold was better. The boys took off for the beach on their bikes, with the men following by car. As soon as Andy was out of sight, Sally squeezed into the front seat of her father's car, next to Mr. Cheyney.

"All right." Mr. Hobbs gave her permission. "After all, it *was* your compass and your matches."

The boat trip took only a few minutes. Once on shore, the boys raced for the cabin. Chuck swung back the sagging door and lifted up the mattress. Bracing his shoulders against it, he reached out for the money box. But the box was not there.

One by one the others joined him, staring with disbelief at the space on the floor where the box was not.

"Oh no," someone groaned.

"Can't be."

"They can't do this to us."

Andy and Chuck each took an end of the mattress and held it high in the air. Bob and Pete shook out the blankets. No box.

Sam, breathing hard, arrived at the shack to find them standing there with sagging shoulders and drooping jaws. "What's the matter?" he puffed.

"No box." Chuck pointed. "You said you put it under the mattress. Well, it's not here now."

With the corners of his mouth curving up, Sam walked over to the wall. He stooped and picked up the box, waving it for them all to see. "We moved the mattress when it rained, dopes. Don't you remember?"

Before the boys could recover from their shock,

178

Sally and the men walked into the room. Proudly Sam placed the box in Mr. Cheyney's hands. Half seriously Bob and Pete clapped.

Crowding around as Mr. Hobbs and Mr. Cheyney counted the money, everyone talked at once.

"How about the reward?"

"Can we get it today?"

"I'm going to buy a boat. Got it all picked out already."

"About the reward." Mr. Hobbs tried to make himself heard. "I think you ought to talk it over with your Den mother and Mr. Thompson. You found this on a Cub project, remember?"

"You mean we should turn the money over to the Cubs and not keep it for ourselves?" Pete demanded. He had spent the morning studying boat catalogues.

"Well, in a way." Mr. Hobbs nodded. "This used to be a wonderful place to camp. Suppose that money was used to buy Gull Island and fix it up? Make it sort of a community picnic and camping place? Probably there'd be enough left to buy a boat, so you wouldn't have to wait for low tide."

"If there isn't enough money left for a boat, *The Enterprise* will help out," Mr. Cheyney promised.

The boys thought it over. "It'll be too hot for playing baseball soon," Chuck figured. He nodded agreement.

Bob followed, then Sam. "Good idea, Dad," Andy finally conceded. "We'll be enjoying the island like you used to."

Pete was the last to say okay. "Just so long as you're sure about the boat."

Straggling back through the underbrush, the boys began to plan improvements for the island. A new fireplace, maybe two lean-tos, a lookout station in the tall oak. As they argued about campsites, Mr. Cheyney tried to hurry them along.

"Come on, boys," he urged. "Got to get back to shore if I'm going to get that extra out today."

"Extra?" Andy almost strangled on the word. "You mean you're going to get out an extra about us?"

"Sure am. The third extra in the history of *The Enterprise*. First when Lincoln was assassinated. Second when the bank was robbed. Third when the money was recovered. You're news, son," and he patted Andy's tousled hair.

The Enterprise was going to print an extra edition about Den Two. Nothing that ever happened was going to be better than today. Andy's chest swelled until it seemed as if it would burst. He opened his mouth to speak, but all he could say was, "Acho-o, acho-o."

12 THE PACK MEETING

The meeting hall began to fill up early the night of the June Pack meeting. Blue-uniformed boys with gleaming shoes and neatly folded yellow kerchiefs slid on the highly polished floor and played tag and leapfrog. Mothers and fathers and small sisters and big brothers seated themselves on the folding chairs which lined the walls. By the time Mr. Thompson's shrill whistle called the room to order at exactly eight o'clock, even the platform in front of the room was crowded.

"Fellows," Mr. Thompson began, "the men you've been working with are visiting us tonight to hear the reports on Know Your Neighborhood. I would like to introduce"—he pointed to the chairs behind him—"Mayor Read, Police Chief Rockey, Fire Chief Whelan, and Mr. Cheyney, editor of *The Enterprise*."

As he mentioned each name there was loud applause. Den Two whistled and stamped their feet when Mr. Cheyney stood up.

"Our other visitor," Mr. Thompson continued, "is connected only indirectly with the project. But he will have something interesting to say later on. Boys, Mr. Oakley of the Huntsville National Bank."

This called for some discussion among the boys on the floor. Applauding politely, neighbor nudged neighbor to lift an eyebrow or whisper, "What's he here for?"

"The reward money, you dope. Our reward." Andy's voice could clearly be heard as he hissed an explanation to Johnny Adams.

Mr. Thompson gave the V signal for silence.

183

"I'm going to run through the awards as quickly as possible. I suggest we cut down on the clapping. There'll be plenty of time for applause later." He smiled in the direction of Den Two and its members sat up straight and beamed at him.

The boys walked forward for their badges and arrows as he called their names. In a loud whisper, Chuck kept score for the Blackhawk Braves. "Sam, Webelos, one run for the home team. Andy, three silver arrows on his Lion, two runs. Me, same, three runs. Bob, two arrows on his Bear, four runs for the home team. Pete, Bear badge and one arrow . . ." Before Mr. Thompson reached the last page of his list, Chuck had seven fingers poked out. "Bases loaded and Jamie up at bat," he chanted. Jamie hunched forward anxiously.

"James Lee, Wolf badge, one silver arrow," Mr. Thompson read.

Chuck's eighth finger shot up. "Another run. All players on the home team scored."

"Good work this month, boys. You've really been in there pitching." Although his words were addressed to everyone, Mr. Thompson seemed to be looking straight at the banner of the Blackhawk Braves. "Now we'll hear the reports. You're first, Den One."

Wearing firemen's hats, Den One slid down imaginary poles and pretended to drive a hook-and-ladder truck. Everyone laughed when little Bill White climbed up on a table and cried, "Help, fire!" until Johnny Adams slung him over his shoulder in a daredevil rescue. At the end, Tom Stein cranked a siren and Johnny threatened to squirt the audience with a real rubber hose.

Den Three acted out their report, too. Don Weber was desk sergeant, sending men off to traffic duty in front of the school and talking to the squad cars over his two-way radio. In a cardboard automobile, painted green and white like the real Huntsville police cars, two boys rode after a speeding car. With their legs plainly visible below the cardboard wheels, they caught the speeder and gave him a ticket. The audience hissed the lawbreaker and stamped their feet for the breathless policemen. Then Don made a speech about crossing streets carefully, and the Den, cupping their hands around

185

their mouths, roared, "Stop, look, and listen."

With questions and answers, just like a quiz program on the radio, Den Four explained the work of the City Council. The mayor himself stepped down from the platform to present a box of candy bars to the Cub who answered most questions correctly.

"Now Den Two," Mr. Thompson announced. "I've saved you for last again. Let's hear what you found at The Enterprise office.

When the room was quiet, Chuck ran down the aisle shouting, "Extra, Extra. Read all about it! Huntsville National Bank robbed!" Trying to keep from laughing, Bob pretended to buy a paper from him. He read aloud the story of the robbery.

"The police were baffled," Andy spoke next. "No trace of the holdup man or the missing money was ever found. Then, two weeks later——"

This was Sam's cue. He stood up to read The Enterprise's account of the body washed up at Tod's Point.

"Twelve years pass," Andy intoned. "The two mysteries have never been solved. The Blackhawk Braves visit the office of The Enterprise and de-

186

termine to find the missing money. With ingen——" As he stumbled over the word, he caught his father's eye and grinned. "With ingenuity and persistence, against great odds and at the peril of their lives——"

Andy waved his arm and Jamie walked across the room piping "Extra, Extra!" as he struggled with a bundle of papers. Pete took one from him to read of the finding of the pay-roll box.

" 'The Case of the Stolen Banknotes has been solved,' " Andy ended with a flourish.

The meeting room rocked with the noise of clapping hands and stamping feet. Motioning for silence, Mr. Thompson asked Mr. Oakley to come forward.

"I'll make this short and sweet," the banker rumbled. "As you all know, we offered a reward for the recovery of the money. It gives me great pleasure to present a check for one thousand dollars to the boys of Den Two. Denner Charles Watson, will you accept this check for your Den?"

Standing as straight as he could, Chuck took the piece of paper Mr. Oakley held toward him. "Pay to the order of Charles Watson. One thousand dollars," he read. "Oh boy!"

"Would you like to tell the Pack what you've decided to do with the reward?" Mr. Thompson suggested.

His cheeks a deep red, Chuck haltingly explained about the purchase of Gull Island and the

plan to turn it into a permanent community recreation center. Then he stumbled to his seat on the floor, waving the check.

While his neighbors crowded around to see it, there was a "Harumph" from the platform. Clearing his throat to catch Mr. Thompson's attention, Chief Rockey stood up. His gold braid and his brass buttons gleamed in the room's bright lights, and his face was as red as Chuck's had been.

"Harumph," he repeated. "This is not my show at all tonight. But I just wanted to say that these boys have done the finest bit of detective work I've

seen in years. Any time they want to come around and teach my men a thing or two, they'll be welcome."

"And now"—Mr. Thompson raised his voice above the applause— "Mr. Cheyney wants to tell you something."

"I just want to warn you, fellows," Mr. Cheyney said with a smile, "that newspaper work is not always as exciting as Den Two manages to make it. Being an editor in a quiet town like Huntsville seldom brings such quick rewards. While I can't compete with Mr. Oakley, *The Enterprise* would like to offer a small treat to you all tonight. Not pie and gingerbread or pigs and slugs." His eyes twinkled. "Just ice cream and soda pop for everyone."

As the boys swarmed toward the refreshment table, Den One put their heads together and shouted:

> "1, 2, 3, 4
> *Who are we for?*
> 5, 6, 7, 8
> *Who do we appreciate?*
> Den Two, Den Two, Den Two!"

The rest of the Pack joined in, cheering their lustiest.

Andy threw an arm around Sam's shoulder and Chuck nudged Bob. "Boy, we slaughtered them," they beamed.